Vintage Sweetheart

Sweetheart Series · Book Three

Shannon Sue Dunlap

Scrivenings
PRESS
Quench your thirst for story.
www.ScriveningsPress.com

Copyright © 2025 by Shannon Sue Dunlap

Published by Scrivenings Press LLC
15 Lucky Lane
Morrilton, Arkansas 72110
https://ScriveningsPress.com

Printed in the United States of America

Paperback ISBN 978-1-64917-533-5

eBook ISBN 978-1-64917-534-2

Editors: Regina Merrick and K. Banks

Cover design by Shannon Sue Dunlap.

To my church family

Chapter One

How could she survive the reunion without a husband?

Deanna Day's eyes crossed at the engagement ring shoved an inch from her nose. Her old classmate, Maryanne Alberta, wiggled her fingers with a squeal. Other women descended on them from every corner of the small second-grade classroom. They crowded around with the appropriate measures of *oohs* and *aahs*.

"He proposed last night." Maryanne held her hand up to the industrial, fluorescent light. "If I'm dreaming, don't wake me! We've been long-distance dating for six months, but he only moved to town three days ago." She giggled. "My man said he couldn't wait any longer."

Lily Wayne jostled Deanna with her elbow. "You should check out online dating. It worked for Maryanne."

Deanna grimaced. "I already tried it once, and it was a complete disaster. I never make the same mistake twice. Besides,"—a smile crossed her lips—"I get plenty of dates, thank you."

"Yes, but none of them last. It's about time you tied the knot like the rest of us."

"Just waiting for the right man."

Maryanne pressed the hand with the ring to her cheek in a pose worthy of a profile picture. "I want you to be as happy as I am, Deanna. You can find a Prince Charming, too. Someone who'll appreciate all the things you've got going for you, like your"—Maryanne tugged the fabric of Deanna's poofy, vintage, polka-dot skirt—"unique fashion sense. And your flair for the dramatic. Stop wasting your time on those community theater shows. You've got to snag somebody before everything starts to sag."

"Maybe I'll surprise you one of these days." Deanna paused and slipped her cell phone from the hidden pocket of her skirt. "Excuse me, y'all." She swiped at the screen and retreated to the large window at the edge of the classroom.

Holding the phone to her ear, she pretended there was an actual voice speaking and threw an occasional "hmm" or "uh-huh" to add believability. All that time she'd spent on the Sweetheart community stage was coming in handy. Perhaps this was an opportunity to talk with someone who might actually answer.

"Dear Lord," she muttered, "why has my life turned out this way? Why does everyone else get the engagement rings? It's not like I haven't tried. You've seen how many dates I've been on. But it was always the wrong man. When are You going to send the right one?"

She traded the phone for a mirror from the same pocket and perused her appearance. The old-fashioned victory rolls she'd swept her hair into were holding firm, and her smile beamed. Not a trace of pique showed on her face. Her polished outer façade hid the fact that inside, she was a shriveled raisin. Was there a prescription for unhappiness? Something to take the edge off the bitter, uninspired succession of sameness each new day brought?

New day?

Deanna scoffed. There was nothing new in her life. She'd lived in the same small town for thirty-three years. Residing in the same house where her parents had brought her home from the hospital. Sleeping in the same daybed she'd used since she was fifteen.

The October trees outside the window burned with autumn glory. Red and orange and harvest-gold colors painted an undeniable signal that change was coming. How she envied them.

Deanna didn't want to leave Sweetheart. She loved it here. But was it too much to ask for her life to finally enter a new season? The endless mediocrity of her existence pressed in on her.

"Deanna!" Lily called from a distance. "Come and see Emmalynn's new baby pictures."

Deanna cringed. Three deep, calming breaths. Inhale through the nose. Exhale through the mouth. She could do this for a few more hours. Hours? A tiny whimper escaped her lips.

She cast a glance around the familiar classroom—another testament to how far her life hadn't come. It felt like only a few years ago that she'd been sitting in one of those second-grade desks, with her best friend, Katherine Bruno, in front of her. And far away on the front row, the boy with the bluest eyes. Evan Colter. Always turning to point those addictive azure pools her way, as if he knew she'd be watching. And she was. She'd followed him like a puppy from the day they were born. Their mothers had delivered them hours apart in the same hospital. She'd pestered him with the same words from the time she learned to talk: *Someday you're gonna marry me.*

She'd spoken those words on the last day she'd seen him,

before Evan and his mother had snuck out of town without telling anyone. The memory pricked her. Deanna looked out the window again, wishing once more for escape.

"Hey, Dee." Katherine slipped alongside, smoothing her knit shirt across her baby bump. "What are you staring at?"

"The past."

Her friend squinted at the window. "Are you speaking metaphorically? All I see is the parking lot."

"Stop teasing. You know I always get sentimental at these events."

"Not just events. Everything. You even cry at animal shelter commercials."

"Hey,"—Deanna nudged her ever so gently—"those abandoned puppy stories are heartrending."

A large white truck with shiny silver rims pulled into the school lot and drove to a space at the end of a row. The driver's door opened, and a man in jeans and a cream sweater emerged. The soft cable-knit fabric stretched over broad shoulders.

Deanna's interest sparked. The benefit of living in a small town like Sweetheart was recognizing all the handsome men in her age range. But this guy was a stranger. His golden-brown hair dipped onto his forehead as he bent to brush the toe of his boot. Could he be the aforementioned future husband of Maryanne Alberta? She'd hit the jackpot.

He stalled at the rear of the truck and ran a hand down his short-trimmed beard, indecision evident in his jerky movements. He turned to the cab, stopped, and rotated again. His chest rose and fell. It appeared Deanna wasn't the only one practicing her deep breathing exercises. Maybe this man realized the endless engagement stories awaiting him inside.

"Run while you can," she muttered.

"Who's that?" Katherine asked.

"I don't know. But there's something familiar about him."

The stranger started toward the building again. As he passed the window, his gaze met Deanna's. Her heart stuttered under her rib cage. She knew those eyes.

Azure blue.

"It can't be," she whispered.

"What?" Katherine leaned closer to the window.

The man halted. His posture tightened, and he spun on his heel, then headed back toward his truck.

"Wait!" Deanna hollered as if he could hear her through the glass. She bolted from the room, bumping into classmates in her haste. Racing through the hallway, she exited the main glass double doors and careened down the sidewalk.

Clip-clop. Clip-clop.

Why had she worn ankle-strap high heels? They were hindering her progress, but she couldn't kick them off.

He was at his truck, his key in the lock. The door opened, and he placed one foot on the running board.

"Evan Colter!" she shouted.

He paused. Turned.

Deanna clip-clopped across the parking lot as fast as her ungainly shoes would allow. Stopping in front of him, she pressed trembling fingers to her chest and gasped for air.

Did he even recognize her? It had been twenty years since they'd seen each other. But what did it matter? He was here.

"Evan Colter," she whispered. Joy shot up inside of her like an elementary school water fountain. Deanna threw her arms around his waist and clung tight. "Welcome home."

Chapter Two

Evan's arms remained trapped under the embrace of the petite blonde who'd chased him down in the parking lot. He didn't have to ask who she was. He knew.

Deanna Day.

They'd grown up together. She'd followed him around since they were old enough to walk. And from the time she could form sentences, she'd declared to anyone who would listen that she was going to marry him someday.

The fact that she was the first person to greet him seemed almost ordained. He'd expected to see her, but he hadn't expected her to practically tackle him to the pavement.

The last time they'd met, she was thirteen years old. Deanna hadn't grown too much since then. Her short arms didn't quite reach all the way around him. A patch of moisture seeped through the material of his sweater. He ducked his head to get a closer look.

Yep. Tears soaked her cheeks. She was still a softy. He might have hugged her if she hadn't been holding him so tight.

"Hello, Dee."

She sniffled and held him tighter, if that was even possible. "Evan Colter, I've missed you like crazy."

He hadn't cried since he was sixteen years old. But Evan found himself swallowing a knot in his throat. Could it really be this easy?

On a whim, he'd searched for the town's newspaper on the internet. To his surprise, *The Sweetheart Clarion* had an online version, and the lead story told about the retirement of the local, longtime second-grade teacher, Mrs. Clara Beauregard. The school was throwing a party-slash-reunion in her honor and had invited all the students she'd taught through the years. He'd agonized for weeks about whether or not to attend. Mrs. Beauregard had always been one of his favorite teachers. And it was a great excuse to visit his old hometown. But a part of him had quaked at the thought.

Would people dredge up the past and his father's misdeeds? Would they tell Evan he wasn't welcome in this town anymore? Would they throw him out?

If Deanna's reaction was any indication, he'd worried for nothing. Why hadn't he returned sooner?

Evan squirmed his arms free from Deanna's death grip, took her by the shoulders, and gently pushed her away a few inches. "Hey, you're getting my best sweater wet."

She sniffled and stared at him with watery eyes. "I can't help it. I've prayed for years that you'd come home, and here you are—in the living, breathing flesh." She released him and smacked his chest hard. "What took you so long?"

"Sorry." He rubbed the stinging spot. "I didn't have the guts to come back."

She didn't ask him what he meant. It must have been obvious. The gloomy specter of his scandalous past followed him.

Deanna pulled him toward the school. "Let's go inside and tell everyone the good news."

He skidded to a halt. "What good news?" His arm stretched between them as she continued to pull.

"That it's time to kill the fatted calf. The prodigal has come home!"

Prodigal? A fitting moniker for his world-weary soul. But he wasn't so sure the good citizens of Sweetheart would throw him a party when he walked through the door.

Chapter Three

Evan stood off to the left of the punch bowl, an empty cup in his hand, and Deanna at his side. After her enthusiastic announcement to the entire room of his return, folks headed over to greet him in an awkward trickle. The response was tepid at best. Mrs. Beauregard hugged him and reminisced about how he was the best student she'd ever had. But a lot of people uttered a few polite commonalities and scurried away.

His old classmate Katie Bruno approached with a man he didn't recognize. She extended her hand. "Long time no see, Evan. I imagine it was hard for you to come back, but I'm glad you did."

The man beside her and Deanna groaned in unison. "Katherine."

Evan paused a second but then shook the brunette's hand and chuckled. "You haven't changed much, Katie. Still as blunt as ever."

"I apologize for my wife." Katie's companion placed his arm around her. "I think this second pregnancy has amplified her, shall we say, tendency to speak the truth."

"The truth is," she jumped in, "I go by Katherine now. Katherine Park. This is my husband, Ryan."

"Nice to meet you." Evan shook the stranger's hand. "How did you two get together?"

Deanna laughed. "They were mortal enemies in opposing mayoral campaigns. Lanette Johnson decided to run against her husband for the office, and these two were their managers. Now look at them. A baby at home and another on the way."

"No kidding." It sounded like Evan had missed a lot in the years he'd been gone. He'd known Harry Johnson became the mayor after Evan's father went to prison, but somehow, the idea that abrasive Lanette had run against her own husband didn't surprise him. "Who won?"

Deanna leaned close with a stage whisper. "Katherine won."

"What?"

"She received the most votes as a write-in candidate and has been the mayor for over two years now. Do you remember the old Sweetheart Memorial Bank? She spearheaded the efforts to convert it into a new town hall. You have to check out what they've done with the place. It's beautiful."

Evan feigned interest in the details while his stomach churned like a fan belt on an old clunker. The mayoral twist of the conversation was dangerous. That was the position his father had held. The one his father took advantage of. Was the same thought running through all of their minds?

After a few minutes, the couple bid goodbye and walked away. Deanna refilled her cup at the punch bowl, and Evan cast a surreptitious glance around the room. A few people stared at him as they whispered. He could just imagine what they were saying.

Evan Colter. I remember him. Didn't his daddy rob the town blind?

You know the old saying—like father, like son.

Bless his heart. How did he have the nerve to show up here?

Deanna slipped in front of him, blocking out the rest of the room with her smile. "Have I mentioned how thrilled I am to see you? I may do a little happy dance." She twirled in one spot. The old-fashioned dress she wore swirled to reveal a crinkly pink slip underneath.

Her unabashed enthusiasm was infectious. It quieted his stomach and allowed an answering grin to creep across his face. "Only about twenty times."

"That's it?" She tsk-tsked. "Expect to hear it at least twenty more before we leave."

Evan laughed. "You always were the kind who made her point."

"I promise you, I haven't changed a bit."

"Oh, I don't know about that," a male voice drawled.

The pair turned to find a lanky cowboy behind them. He wore a black Stetson, a long-sleeved pearl snap shirt tucked into a pair of crisp blue jeans, and a large, silver belt buckle with an engraving of a bucking bronco. He looked like he'd ambled out of a cheap late-night television western.

"Boone!" Deanna grabbed him by the arm and drew him closer. "You remember Evan. We attended school together."

"Evan Colter." The tall man stuck his thumbs behind his buckle and peered down his nose. "How could I forget?"

Evan didn't relish having to stare up, but Boone topped him by a good four or five inches. It was probably the cowboy boots. Was he imagining the antagonism in the other man's glare?

Evan held out a hand. "Good to see you again."

Boone made no move to shake it. "Been a long time, Colter. What you been up to?"

He lowered his hand. "This and that. I live in Dallas now."

"Good."

"Boone, behave yourself," Deanna hissed. "Evan isn't familiar with your sense of humor. He might take it the wrong way."

The man's cheeks reddened, and he tugged at his hat. "Pardon me, Evan. Hope you enjoy your visit. How long are you plannin' to stay?"

Something about the question goaded him. Or was it the eager tone Boone used when he referred to Evan's departure? Either way, it brought out Evan's ornery side.

"I'm not sure. It's been a long time since I've been home."

"Too long." Deanna's head bobbed like a fishing lure. "You should stick around awhile. A long while."

Boone harumphed. Angling his body Deanna's direction, a bright smile appeared on his face. "Are we still on for dinner Friday night?"

She quirked an eyebrow. "Only if you promise not to propose again."

"Again?" Evan asked.

"You know what they say." Boone hooked his thumbs in the waist of his jeans. "Third time's a charm."

"Not in my case." Deanna poked Evan with a conspiratorial elbow. "How many times did I ask you to marry me? Fifty? A hundred?"

Evan rubbed his bearded chin as if it were hard to calculate. "Considering you used to end all your dinner prayers with 'and please let me marry Evan when I grow up,' I imagine it was more than a hundred."

"My bedtime prayers, too. The Good Lord took pity on me and decided to fulfill my childhood dream." She slipped her arm back around his. "To walk down the aisle with Evan Colter."

"Wh—I—" Boone sputtered.

Evan cast an exasperated look Deanna's way. The answering twinkle in her eye told him she was enjoying the ticklish situation she'd orchestrated.

"Deanna Day!" A sharp voice exclaimed. An older woman with unnaturally red hair bustled up behind them. "Don't tell me you're finally getting married!"

Deanna whirled so fast the punch sloshed out of her cup and landed on her skirt. "Oh no," she wailed.

Evan crumpled his empty cup. The brazen interrupter made his bones freeze. He may have forgotten a lot of people, but he still remembered this woman. Even twenty years ago, Mrs. Biddle was the biggest gossip in town.

Chapter Four

I've stepped in a cow patty this time. Haven't I, Lord?

Deanna supposed she deserved whatever interrogation was coming. What had possessed her to kid around about marrying Evan Colter? And at the worst possible moment! The burgundy-topped woman standing before them caused more rumor storms in Sweetheart than the entire Ladies Auxiliary combined.

Mrs. Biddle took gossip to an art form.

The woman's intrusive gaze didn't miss a detail as she studied the two of them from head to toe. Deanna longed to bolt. She peeked at the classroom. Mrs. Beauregard sat thumbing through an old yearbook at the teacher's desk, Maryanne Alberta was flashing her ring under someone else's nose, and people talked in cheerful groups, clueless to the Greek tragedy happening at the punch bowl.

As if Deanna hadn't felt pathetic enough being the only single woman at the party, now she would have to admit she was making up fake engagements. She shifted to the side so her body was half hidden behind Evan's taller frame. He stood rigid, his face an impassive mask.

Mrs. Biddle batted her lashes. "A secret romance! Deanna, you're a sly little miss. How did you hide this from me? When did you two reconnect?"

"That's what I want to know." Boone Richardson shoved into the group. "You and I went on a date two weeks ago. Since when are you marrying him?"

Deanna gave a weak laugh. "What can I say? You never forget your childhood sweetheart."

"But when?" Mrs. Biddle focused her attention on Evan. "Was it a long-distance thing? Did you meet a few months ago when Deanna took that trip to Dallas? Do your parents know? I heard Evan's father got out of jail. What's he doing these days?"

"Mrs. Biddle!" Deanna interrupted the machine-gun queries.

"What?" The old woman's thirsty expression telegraphed her unquenchable curiosity.

Evan remained silent during the onslaught of questions. He looked at Deanna, his bearded jawline stiff as a stone wall.

She fidgeted and rubbed at the pink stain on her skirt. "What a mess." And she wasn't just talking about the fruit punch. "How can I clean this up?"

Evan shifted. "I'll get you some paper towels." He walked away without ever speaking directly to Mrs. Biddle.

Deanna envied him the excuse. Why hadn't she thought of it first? She gulped and flinched at the old gossip, who was poking Boone with a purple-tipped fingernail.

"Guess you missed the boat, young man. You snooze, you lose."

He jerked away. "I don't see a ring on Deanna's finger. Until that happens, there's still hope."

"Good point." The purple fingernail waggled at Deanna.

"It's not official until the man gets down on one knee. Has he given you a proper proposal yet? Or is this one of those maybe-we'll-get-around-to-it-someday engagements?"

Deanna's cheeks burned. "Mrs. Biddle, I—I was the one who said we're getting married. Evan hasn't—"

"Makes no nevermind who does the proposing." Mrs. Biddle waved her hand. "If he agreed, it's still binding. Don't let him weasel out of it. Evan was a good boy when he was younger, but you can't discount genetics. If he takes after his father, you might need to keep an eye on him."

Boone nodded. "The apple doesn't fall far from the tree."

Deanna clamped her back molars tight. "Stop it," she ground out. "Neither of you knows anything about Evan. He's returned home after an eternity, and you should be welcoming him with open arms, not making mean-spirited accusations."

"Mean-spirited?" Mrs. Biddle pressed her chest. "Why, Deanna Day. That's no way to speak to your elders."

"And what *you* said is no way to speak to anyone. If you repeat your vicious comments when Evan gets back,"—Deanna glared at Boone—"either of you, I promise I'll throw a fit bigger than this classroom has ever seen."

"De-aaaaana," Boone whined.

"I'm serious as a speeding ticket."

Mrs. Biddle fanned her face. "My, my. Who knew you and Evan were writing your own romance novel? Your devotion is too precious for words."

Katherine joined their group and passed Deanna a fistful of paper towels. "Here, Dee. Before Evan left, he asked me to give you these."

"He's gone?" Deanna clenched the towels.

"I suppose so. He walked out the door a few minutes ago, holding his car keys."

Panic crashed through Deanna. It took two decades to meet Evan again, and he'd slipped away without so much as a goodbye. Just like the first time.

What if he never came back?

Mrs. Biddle smirked. "Guess I was right when I said you'd better keep an eye on him."

Chapter Five

Deanna peered out the large glass window of the soda fountain–museum she ran for her mother. The main street of Sweetheart, Texas, was even sleepier than usual on this bright Saturday morning. She'd opened early in the hopes she might spot Evan driving by. If he was even still in town.

"Stupid." She wasn't sure if she meant Evan or herself. The word applied to both of them. Evan was stupid for leaving last night without telling her. And for leaving without telling her the first time. And for staying away so long. Deanna was stupid for letting him out of her sight for even a moment. She should have kept a death grip on his arm until she at least obtained a current phone number. They needed to talk. Talk about what had changed and how he'd been and what his plans were and … and the painful past. If he'd stuck around five minutes longer, she might have mustered the courage to confess something she'd been wanting to tell him for twenty years.

A bitter sigh escaped her lips. From childhood on, it seemed like her romance with Evan Colter was doomed to failure. Deanna stalked behind the long wooden bar that held the soda fountain. She fussed with the empty pill drawers on the wall as she had for the past ten years. They'd been left from when the building was an old drugstore. Now she hid her makeup, hairpins, sunglasses, and more in them.

The bell attached to the entrance jingled, and Aunt Lanette cannonballed into the museum. Her friend Elise Walker scurried behind her.

"Hey, Aunt Lanette." Deanna swerved around the counter.

"Don't you 'Hey, Aunt Lanette' me, ungrateful girl." The woman who'd been like a second mother to Deanna halted in the middle of the room with her hands on her hips. She tapped her hot pink nails against her bedazzled blue jeans. Her blonde head vibrated in indignation. "I know we don't share any real blood, but I always considered us family."

Deanna grabbed a feather duster and fluttered it along a display of vintage hats. What was the issue this time? Aunt Lanette's passionate nature meant she spent many days ecstatic or outraged but rarely calm. "We *are* family."

"Then why do I hear from Cora Biddle that you're getting married? I should have been the first call after you told your mother."

Deanna froze. "Who's getting married?"

"You, silly." Elise poked her head over the shorter Lanette's shoulder. Her hairstyle was an exact copy of her friend's, except for the silver-gray color. "Congratulations, by the way. Are you going to have a church wedding?"

Aunt Lanette stormed to the counter, plopped on a stool, and crossed her arms. "Cora banged on my front door at six this morning. A phone call wouldn't do. She had to come by in person and pester me for all the particulars. You can imagine her unmitigated delight when she discovered she knew more about the situation than me."

"Me too." Deanna tossed the duster next to a collection of

velvet fascinators. "I missed the proposal entirely. Did Mrs. Biddle happen to mention the name of the groom?"

"You don't know?" Elise's eyes widened. "It's—"

"Hold on." Aunt Lanette raised a rigid palm. "Are you getting married or not?"

"Absolutely." Deanna glanced in a gilt-edged mirror sitting near the hats and fussed with her drooping pin curls. "But I need someone to ask me first."

"I knew it!" Aunt Lanette laughed. "I knew my girl couldn't be that cruel, to make me find out about her wedding from the town gossip."

Elise scooted on the stool beside her. "Poor Evan. I wonder if he knows he's not marrying you."

"Evan?" Deanna froze for the second time. She stared at Elise's reflection in the mirror. "You mean Evan Colter?"

"Yep."

Aunt Lanette's lips pulled to the side in disgust. "Cora drank three cups of coffee while describing your romantic reunion at the school last night. It baffles me how that woman can be so nosy and misinformed at the same time. If you didn't say you were marrying Evan, I wonder how she got the idea."

Deanna faced them. "Well—I did say that. Sort of. But I wasn't making an official announcement. It was a joke. And Mrs. Biddle was across the room at the time. Evan never proposed."

Elise tsk-tsked. "You can't make those kinds of remarks around Cora Biddle. She's got the hearing of a bird dog."

"And the imagination of a Hollywood screenwriter." Lanette shook her head. "She can create an epic blockbuster from one throwaway comment."

Deanna walked to the empty stool beside Aunt Lanette. She sat and twisted to adjust the stiff nylon crinoline under her skirt. It scratched at her legs like the thoughts in her brain.

Did anyone else in Sweetheart think she was marrying Evan?

If Mrs. Biddle had anything to do with it, yes.

Deanna checked her antique cocktail watch. Eleven o'clock. The whole town knew by now.

Wait.

If the whole town knew, that meant Evan knew. Right? Deanna squeezed her eyes shut and groaned. How humiliating.

Maybe he'd left before the gossip started. He was probably already back in Dallas. But was that a good thing or a bad thing? When he'd gone to fetch some paper towels, there'd been no indication he was leaving town. Then again, he might not have entered the party if she hadn't grabbed him in the parking lot.

Now that he was out of tackling distance, would she ever see him again?

E van rolled down his truck window and took a deep breath, relishing the crisp, clean smell. Not even the slightest hint of gasoline fumes or fried fast food. He'd missed this. If only he could stick around awhile.

Familiar buildings sped by as he drove out of town. He'd spent the night at a bed-and-breakfast run by a married couple who'd lived in Sweetheart a mere three years. They'd known nothing of his family scandal and treated him like any other guest by offering up flowery, romanticized tales of the history of Sweetheart. Considering it was Evan's great-great-grandfather who'd founded the town, it was a bit of a stretch to act surprised with each story.

He passed the city limits sign that declared a population of five thousand seven people, a far cry from his current abode. The Dallas–Fort Worth metroplex boasted over seven million residents. Evan should be used to the noise and crowding and terrible drivers, but he still hated it.

"I guess my small-town roots are buried deep," he murmured to himself.

A well-worn gravel lane appeared ahead. His foot let off the gas pedal, and his hand automatically turned the steering wheel. Would the old place still look the same? He might be asking for trouble visiting the Colters' ranch. It had been sold to the Hammington family years ago to help pay his father's court costs. Although Mr. Hammington was gone, his widow had been less than receptive to Evan's phone calls offering to buy the property.

He drove under the wrought iron sign suspended from a tall entryway. It still read Double Heart Ranch, the name his great-great-grandfather, Amos Colter, gave the place in honor of his bride. Family tradition had it that great-great-grandma had required quite a bit of wooing, and Amos had tried just about everything to impress her. The familiar curves and grooves of the metal letters were a reminder of what Evan had lost. His family honor. His roots. Himself.

He pulled the truck to a stop in front of the house and killed the engine. Rolling green pastures surrounded the place with lopsided three-rail fencing that had seen better days. The one-story homestead needed a paint job, and holes in the wraparound porch gaped like missing teeth. To the left side of the house sat the huge barn he used to play in as a child. Half the shingles were missing from the roof, and one door hung sideways off its hinges. Everywhere he looked, there was something in need of repair. Grandma Colter must be rolling in her grave.

Could he turn back the clock for the ranch? And for himself?

He grabbed a pile of papers from the passenger seat. Attending the reunion had been only one of the reasons for traveling to Sweetheart. Marjorie Hammington hadn't been very receptive when he'd called from Dallas, but maybe appealing to her face-to-face would make a difference.

Evan exited the truck. He squared his shoulders, made his

way up the front walk, and knocked on the door. A long silence was followed by shuffling on the other side. The click of two deadbolts and sliding rattle of a chain lock preceded the door opening a crack.

"Who is it?" A suspicious hazel eye peeked out at him.

"Hello, Mrs. Hammington. It's me. Evan Colter." He moved away to give her a better view.

"Evan Colter?" The older woman swung the door wider and squinted at him. Her thinning gray hair stuck out on the left side of her head, a floral housecoat stretched to her knobby knees, and a pair of threadbare pink fuzzy slippers covered her feet. "What on earth are you doing here?"

"I wanted to talk to you about selling the ranch."

Mrs. Hammington crossed her skinny arms over the flower print. "I already told you when you called, I wasn't interested."

"I know. And I'm sorry to be a pest. But"—he scratched his beard—"I was hoping you might change your mind."

She sniffed. "Where am I supposed to live if I sell this place to you?"

He rustled the papers in his hand. "I did research on the internet before I came. There are several nice houses available in town. It would be more convenient when you do your shopping, and there'd be a lot less property to look after." He motioned to the ramshackle porch. "I imagine it's a headache keeping up with five hundred acres."

She glared at the papers. "Not as much of a headache as packing twenty years of junk and moving."

"If it's the packing that bothers you, I'd be willing to help." Evan smiled and took an eager step forward. "All you have to do is point, and I'll box every dinner plate and knick-knack. Transport is included."

"You've called me more than once about this. Why can't you take no for an answer?" Mrs. Hammington finally uncrossed her arms. "I reckon a man gets desperate when he wants to start a family."

His smile faltered. "A family?"

"Cora Biddle called me this morning and told me all about how you're marrying that pretty little Deanna Day. 'Bout time she settled down. There's hardly an eligible man in the town she hasn't dated."

"Mrs. Biddle?" He ruffled his hair. "I don't understand. Dee and I aren't—I mean, I never told Mrs. Biddle—"

Mrs. Hammington cackled. "Oh, you don't have to tell Cora anything. She digs up the dirt on her own. Although the news surprised me, I must admit, the thought of a young couple living here again does something to me. Reminds me of when my husband and I were starting out. The Double Heart Ranch was meant to have two people who love each other living here." She took the papers from his limp hand. "Come inside and drink a cup of coffee while we talk about it." With a soft expression, she steadied herself on the doorjamb.

Evan stared at her with panicked eyes. Should he tell the woman there'd been a mistake? Some old busybody had spread false information. He ought to correct the lies. But unlike when he'd called on the phone, Mrs. Hammington sounded as if she might entertain his offer to buy the ranch. How could he just throw that opportunity away?

She tapped a slippered foot. "Are you coming in or not?"

He cleared his throat. "I—I'm so grateful you're willing to consider my offer, Mrs. H. But as far as Dee and I are concerned—"

A rattling sounded.

The older woman craned her neck to see over his shoulder. "Look who's here."

Evan glanced behind him as a light-blue, vintage Schwinn bicycle bumped along the gravel drive. Sitting atop was a woman appearing like she'd ridden out of a 1950s catalog advertisement, complete with giant sunglasses and an animal print scarf wrapped around her hair with the silk ends fluttering in the wind.

A bony elbow poked Evan in the gut, and Mrs. Hammington grinned up at him. "Got Deanna to help you talk me into it, huh?"

The classic bike rattled to the house. Deanna dismounted in a poofy, white, sleeveless dress with matching gloves. She reached back to the cargo rack and untied a cardboard box with mason jar lids peeking from the top.

"Hello, girlie." Mrs. Hammington waved.

"Evan!" The newcomer practically skipped down the walk and joined them on the porch. "What are you doing here?"

Should he admit he was trying to buy the ranch or just give up and leave? "I-I was—"

"Oh, don't even bother pretending." Mrs. Hammington swatted the girl on the arm. "Like you didn't know he was here."

"I promise I didn't." Deanna extended the box. "Momma asked me to bring you a few jars of her homemade apple butter."

"Trying to butter me up, huh?" The old woman cackled and swung her arm to the inside of the house. "Well, you two lovebirds come in. I ain't promising anything, but I'll at least hear you out." She hobbled away without a backward glance.

Deanna removed her sunglasses. "'Lovebirds'?"

Evan pressed both hands to the top of his head, elbows cocooning his face. This was crazy. Why had Cora Biddle invented such a ridiculous story?

"You haven't heard?" he asked. "Mrs. Biddle told everyone we're getting married."

"Actually"—her gaze dropped—"I did hear. This morning, at least five people stopped by to offer their congratulations."

"Did you tell them I'd proposed?" He dropped his hands to his sides.

"Of course not!" She glared up at him. "Other than the joking remark I made at the reunion, I haven't said a word. But it doesn't take much to get Mrs. Biddle's gossip motor churning."

He blew a frustrated breath from tense lips. "Great. Now what?"

Her answering silence underlined the pickle they were in.

Evan grunted. "Exactly."

Deanna pulled the scarf from her hair and tucked it in her pocket. "Why are you here?"

"I've been asking Mrs. H to sell me this place. It was my great-great-grandfather's old homestead."

"Yes, I know. But I thought you just got back in town yesterday."

"I did. But I've called her a few times in the past to test the waters. She turned me down cold whenever I suggested it. Today was the first sign of her weakening, but it's because she believes we're getting married."

Deanna shifted the box, and the glass jars clinked against each other.

He took it from her with a sigh. "Come on, Dee. Let's tell her the truth and see if she's still willing to consider my offer."

Deanna raised a skeptical eyebrow. "What do you think the chances are?"

"Slim to none. But I've got to try. It's important to me."

Chapter Seven

S helves of teddy bears lined the rough wooden walls of the living room. Dust covered the picture frames on the fireplace mantel. A TV tray with empty glasses sat by the armchair, and a hodgepodge of medicine bottles covered the coffee table. Mrs. Hammington skirted the miscellaneous items with well-acquainted ease and motioned Evan and Deanna to the couch. Deanna's skirt brushed a waist-high stack of magazines as she moved, and they toppled to the floor.

"I'm so sorry!" She scrambled to retrieve them.

"Don't worry about it." Mrs. Hammington settled on a dilapidated recliner and rested her head on the crocheted doily covering the head cushion. "When you get to be my age, it's too much trouble to put things away."

Deanna collected the crinkled magazines. Evan set the box of apple butter on the lone empty spot on the coffee table and bent to help her. Together, they made quick work of cleaning up the mess and sat on the sofa across from Mrs. Hammington. A huge pile of unfolded laundry on one end forced them to huddle close.

Evan's sleeve pressed against Deanna's bare arm. The heat

of his body distracted her. It was hard to believe that, after all these years, her childhood sweetheart was sitting next to her. Not that she'd been *his* sweetheart. More like the bratty younger sister tagging along whether he wanted it or not.

If Evan could convince Mrs. Hammington to sell the ranch, that meant he might stick around awhile. She had to help him. Her one goal in life from the time she was five years old was to marry Evan Colter. And that would be a lot easier to accomplish if they were in the same town.

Deanna tugged her now-dusty gloves from her fingers and started to fold a large terry cloth towel. "You've got your plate full with such a big place, Mrs. Hammington."

The woman's right nostril wrinkled. "What's the point of putting the laundry away? There's nobody here but me to see it."

"If you sell this place," Evan said, "I'll find a nice house for you in town. You can be closer to your friends and the church and—"

Deanna jumped in. "And the Ladies Auxiliary card nights. You love those."

Mrs. Hammington squinted at Evan. "What was it you said on the phone? You want to turn my house into a hotel?"

"Not a hotel." He propped his elbows on his knees. "A boys' ranch for troubled youth."

"I didn't know that." Deanna rotated his direction. "What made you think of it?"

Mrs. Hammington leaned forward to hear his answer.

Evan's cheeks colored. "It's a long story. But there are so many boys who'd benefit. They can get away from the city and bad influences, learn to work the land, and experience how it feels to live with a purpose."

"Wow." Moisture filled Deanna's eyes.

It was such a beautiful dream. She envied him. Not even

once in her life had she settled on something she wanted to devote herself to. Except for Evan, of course.

Mrs. Hammington nodded. "It's a worthwhile plan. I suppose you and Deanna would live here in the main house."

"Me and——" Evan blinked.

Deanna laid a warning hand on his forearm. "Does that mean you'll consider his offer?"

"Don't push me, girlie." The older woman chuckled. "You must be in a hurry to move in and set up housekeeping. I was the same way at your age. Couldn't wait to be Mrs. Hammington." Her cloudy gaze drifted to the mantelpiece. On it sat a picture of her in a long white dress with flowers in her beehive hair, a tall, somber man in a dress suit at her side. "Next week is our sixtieth wedding anniversary."

Evan cocked his head. "I thought your husband passed aw——"

Deanna pinched his back.

Mrs. Hammington eyed him. "Just because my man's gone to be with Jesus doesn't mean I can't celebrate one of the best things that ever happened to me. I'll keep counting our anniversaries until I see him again."

Deanna's tears returned in full force. "That's wonderful. I bet Mr. Hammington is remembering your anniversary in Heaven."

She scoffed. "He never remembered it on Earth. I imagine it would take the Good Lord Himself to remind him now. Marvin Hammington wasn't the romantic type. Most men aren't, you know." She pointed a wrinkled finger at Evan. "Don't forget the special days. Try to spoil Deanna a little."

Evan shifted on the couch. "Mrs. Hammington, there's been a misunderstanding. I'm not——"

"Oh sure. Every man thinks he's the exception. He'll bring a truckload of flowers and candy before the wedding. But after the *I do*s are done, it's a different story. Marvin and I lived and loved and fought our way through every single room in this house, including the attic." She sighed. "It's time for another couple to fill it with memories."

Evan cringed. "We're not a—"

"You'll sell the ranch?" Deanna bolted from her seat, propelled around the coffee table, and threw her arms around Mrs. Hammington. "Thank you, thank you!"

She laughed and made a half-hearted effort to push her away, but Deanna clung tight. The fragile hands settled on her back and patted.

Mrs. Hammington's tone wobbled. "I'm very happy for you, girlie."

It was a good thing the older woman couldn't observe Deanna's face. A wave of panic hit her. She'd been caught up in the moment as if it were true. Her enthusiasm for helping Evan had overridden her common sense. But this plan was better for everyone involved. Mrs. Hammington would be safer in town, Evan would move to Sweetheart, and his ranch would change the lives of countless troubled youth.

Deanna pulled away. "Once everything is final, I'll dash here lickety-split to help you pack stuff up." She crossed the room and gestured to the stuffed animals lining the wall. "It'll take a whole moving truck for your teddy bear collection alone."

"Mercy me, I'm not taking those things." Mrs. Hammington popped the lever on the side of her recliner and raised the footrest. "Somehow, word got around I liked teddy bears, and that's all I got as gifts for the last twenty years. I'll be thrilled to get rid of them."

Deanna laughed. "Then we'll help you find a good home for them. Right, Ev—" She paused at his shell-shocked demeanor. Poor guy. It had been a while since he'd experienced what folks in town jokingly referred to as Hurricane Deanna. She walked to him and took him by the arm. "Come on, honey. We'll let Mrs. Hammington take a nap and iron out the details later."

"I—I—"

The elderly woman's lids drooped.

Evan blew out an exasperated breath. "Let's go."

They tiptoed through the cluttered living room, down the hall to the exit, and gently closed the front door behind them. The second they stepped on the porch, Evan rounded on her.

"Am I going insane?" He pressed his fingers to his temples. "We conned that woman out of her ranch."

"What are you talking about?" Deanna propped her hands on her hips. "She wanted to sell. I can sense these things. All she needed was a little push."

"We can't keep lying." His face pointed at the floor, almost as if he were lecturing himself. "It wouldn't be right."

"When did we lie to her? She made the assumptions about our engagement. We just didn't correct her."

A hard glint chilled his blue eyes. "You'd make a good politician."

Deanna froze. Unpleasant memories from twenty years ago flooded her mind. His father, standing before the town council, being accused of corruption. The subsequent trial, where Mayor Colter insisted on his innocence until the bitter end despite the overwhelming mountain of evidence and numerous witnesses.

If the wince on Evan's face was any indication, he was reliving the same painful experience.

She placed gentle hands on his arms. "I agree, Evan. Don't worry. I promise we'll tell her soon." She headed for her bicycle and patted the seat cushion. "Help me load this in your truck. You can save me some exercise."

He followed her and lifted the bicycle under one arm. "Why did you pedal all the way out here?"

"I don't drive."

"You don't drive?" He stared at her as if she'd said she didn't bathe. "Why?"

"I've always lived in Sweetheart, and most places are a ten-minute bike ride away. It's only when I come out to Mrs. Hammington's that it gets dicey."

"That makes no sense. It's the twenty-first century. Everyone in this day and age should learn how to drive."

"I'll make you a deal." She bumped him with her hip. "Give me private lessons, and I'll chauffeur you across the state of Texas."

The twitch of Evan's lips signaled his capitulation. He loaded the bike in his pickup, then looked at her with amused resignation. His azure eyes washed over her like a sun-warmed Caribbean wave. It had been so long since she'd reveled in their warmth—too many years wasted.

She'd lost him once, and Deanna never made the same mistake twice. She'd been too young to do anything about it back then, but now it was different. She was a grown woman with a head full of brains and a heart full of love. Whether he knew it or not, Evan Colter was going to marry her.

Chapter Eight

The mealtime buzz in The Brunch Café provided a comfortable cover for a private conversation as Deanna and Evan shared a corner booth. She drew the paper napkin off the cherry red tabletop and spread it on her lap. Evan took a peek over his shoulder like a criminal afraid of being recognized in public.

"Relax," Deanna said. "No one's paying any attention to us. When do you return to Dallas?" She took a drink from her water glass.

"Today."

She spluttered. A spray of water hit Evan. He reared back and wiped his wet cheek.

"Oh!" Deanna grabbed her napkin and leaned across the table. "I-I, I'm so sorry, Evan. You took me by surprise. That's all."

He took the paper from her to dab his face, and she sat stiffly in her seat.

Crater-sized cracks spread through her soul. She couldn't just let him drive off into the sunset. She had to do something.

"You're leaving today? How"—she noted other diners

looking their way and lowered her voice—"how could you even suggest giving up? You were trying to buy the Double Heart Ranch. Doesn't that mean you plan to stay awhile?"

"I considered it." He finished mopping up the water and pushed the napkin to the side. "But I doubt Mrs. Hammington will still want to sell to me once she realizes how we've deceived her."

"Deceive is such an ugly word." Deanna waved her hand. "It's a misunderstanding. I'm sure she'll forgive us when we explain what happened."

Hope lit Evan's eyes. "Do you think so?"

"Absolutely. Mrs. Hammington is sweet as sugar underneath that gruff. As long as we're the ones to tell her and not some random gossip, I'm sure we can make her understand. Especially now that she knows what a glorious plan you have for the property. A boys' ranch will help so many kids! I admit I got a little choked up when you were explaining the idea earlier. It shows what a huge heart you have to think of such a thing."

He picked up the discarded napkin and rubbed at the already dry table. "It's no big deal."

"It's a very big deal. What made you first consider renovating your family's place into a boys' ranch?"

He didn't answer right away. A laugh sounded from the front door as a couple exited. Two older men by the window started fighting about a softball game. The happy noise inside the café clashed with the somber expression on Evan's face.

Deanna laid a hand on top of his. "Evan?"

He pulled away and tossed the napkin on the table. "The reason I want to start a boys' ranch is because I once lived at one."

"You—you lived at a—"

"A rehabilitation center." He raised his chin as if he were steeling himself for her reaction.

A dozen questions sprinted through Deanna's brain, but only one eeked past her lips. "Why?"

"I was"—he licked his lips—"going through a rough patch then. Hanging out with the wrong people. Getting in trouble. One night, I went for a joyride and only found out the car was stolen when the cops pulled us over."

Deanna gasped. "Oh no!"

"Yeah. But in the end, it turned out to be the best thing that ever happened to me. The ranch screwed my head on straight. Who knows where I would have ended up without it? Prison. Or worse."

He avoided her gaze, but Deanna grabbed his hand.

"And now you want to give other boys that same chance. I think that's amazing!"

"Really?" He looked up.

"Absolutely. You can't run away now. No matter how Mrs. Hammington grumbles, I know we can convince her."

He withdrew and crossed his arms tight. "I don't know. Maybe I should just forget the whole thing."

Deanna thumped the table. "Evan Colter, don't you dare disappear again. This is your home, and you're going to stay here."

"Dear me!" A louder-than-necessary voice sounded beside them.

They both turned to find Mrs. Biddle observing them with the somberness of Sherlock Holmes. All that was missing was the magnifying glass.

"Please don't tell me you're quarreling already. That's no way to start an engagement." Suspicion radiated from her. "You *are* engaged, aren't you? I just assumed from what

Deanna said last night at the reunion that the deal was done, but you two don't exactly resemble starry-eyed turtledoves."

"What's with the third degree, Mrs. B?" Deanna fussed with the neckline of her white dress. "The whole town's aware I've always been crazy about Evan."

"Yes, dear. But is he crazy about you?" The older woman scrutinized the man in question.

Deer in the headlights wasn't the exact phrase to describe Evan's expression. More like *squirrel under a semi*. Deanna reached for the hand he'd rested on the table and locked her fingers around it.

She called on her many years of thespian experience in community theater shows to deliver a convincing laugh. "What single man in Sweetheart isn't crazy about me, Mrs. B? I've got them all twisted around my little finger." She waved her pinky for good measure.

"Cora!" The woman behind the register called. "You forgot your change."

"Oh yes." Mrs. Biddle's eyes darted between Evan and Deanna. "Hold that thought."

The moment she left, Evan yanked his hand away and laid both palms flat on the table. "What do we do?"

Deanna nibbled at her lip. "If we admit the truth now, it will get around to Mrs. Hammington before we can confess. You've seen how quick the gossip spreads in Sweetheart. I'd hate for Mrs. Biddle to make Mrs. H feel like a fool. She deserves to hear it from us."

He sighed. "You're right, but how do we get out of this pickle we're in?"

An outrageous brain wave hit Deanna—one she shouldn't even entertain. But it was oh-so-tempting.

She took another drink of water to wet her suddenly

parched throat. "I have an idea, but"—she set the glass on the table—"it's unusual."

"What else is new?" Evan deadpanned. "You haven't done one normal thing since I met you, Deanna Day. And I'm talking about our first meeting, when we were both in diapers."

"I'm glad you understand me so well." She bent closer and lowered her voice. "So how about kissing me?"

"I beg your pardon?"

"Kissing me."

Her gaze cut to Mrs. Biddle, who was surveilling them from the cash register as she accepted the change. Deanna talked faster, knowing they had mere seconds before the nosy woman returned.

"Listen, Mrs. Biddle's imagination could put Hans Christian Andersen to shame. We don't have to go for broke. Just a quick smooch, and I bet she'd race out of here without even bothering to ask us any more questions, and that will buy us some time to visit Mrs. Hammington and explain the"— Deanna ran out of air and stopped for a breath—"the truth."

She recognized the expression on Evan's face. He'd given her the same exasperated look many times when they were kids and she'd suggested another wild adventure. It usually precluded him giving in and letting her have her way. Would history repeat itself?

"Fine," he ground out.

"Really?"

Deanna's jaw slacked. Her heart pounded as if it were announcing to the whole room how excited she was. After all this time, she'd finally get to kiss Evan Colter. Could reality ever live up to almost thirty years of daydreams?

He leaned into her space—his lips an inch from hers. She drew back the slightest bit. Flames lit her cheeks like someone had ignited a gas burner.

"What's the matter?" he whispered. "This was your idea."

She gulped. "True, but—The notion hit me—What if I'm disappointed?"

His brows dipped. "Disappointed?"

"I know it sounds stupid, but ... I've dreamed of kissing you ever since I was five years old. I don't think any man could fulfill that kind of expectation. Not even you."

He chuckled and shook his head. "Way to set me up for failure. Would you rather go home?"

"And leave Mrs. Biddle hot on our trail? No way!" Why had she even brought up any doubts? Now she couldn't unsay the words. What if Evan was offended? What if he hated her after this? What if—

He closed the gap before she finished cataloguing her worries.

His lips settled on hers. Firm. Warm. Delicious.

A spiral began in Deanna's tummy and skyrocketed through her core. It lit a fuse that might have burst into fireworks, but Evan pulled away. He expelled a breath and inclined his head toward the front of the restaurant.

"Do you suppose we convinced her?" he murmured.

Deanna's gaze swung to the woman in question. Mrs. Biddle's eyeballs almost bugged out of her head. Deanna imagined the busybody making a mental list of who she would call.

"Dee." Evan nudged her.

"Hmm?"

"Did we satisfy Mrs. Biddle's curiosity?"

"I imagine so." She sucked the inside of her bottom lip between her teeth and gnawed. Maybe Mrs. Biddle's curiosity was satisfied, but Deanna's was bursting at the seams.

Evan's kiss *had* disappointed her, but not because of the quality. It was the equivalent of one of those taste-testing cups they passed out at the farmer's market to hook passing customers, whetting her appetite for more. What would a *real* kiss from Evan feel like?

His finger tapped her hand. "Mrs. B just zoomed out the front door. Could she be booking a wedding hall for us?"

"Probably picking out names for our children." Deanna's light trill wasn't a genuine laugh. It was the one she'd perfected when she played flighty Lydia in the high school production of *Pride and Prejudice*.

The menus rested between the silver napkin dispenser and the wall. She slipped one out and raised it to block her face. As one of this establishment's most devoted patrons, she hardly needed to study it. What she needed was a moment to compose herself. If only the plastic-covered list gave suggestions for what to say after suckering a guy into laying one on her. Kissing Evan had been the top item on her to-do list for decades, and the reality had surpassed her dreams by a country mile. But now that she'd mentally crossed it off, a new goal immediately took its place.

To kiss Evan Colter every day for the rest of her life.

Chapter Nine

E van stared at the plastic barrier Dee had erected between them. A laugh swelled in his throat. He'd worried for years what would happen if he returned to Sweetheart, but never in his wildest dreams had he considered kissing Deanna Day less than twenty-four hours after hitting town. She was the bratty little sister who'd followed him around his whole childhood.

Bratty but adorable.

Even now, he couldn't help smiling at her. She was as artless and passionate as ever. Years of separation had melted away in the fervor of her desire to help him. They were kids again, working together to pull off another impossible scheme.

Fear struck that he might unintentionally hurt her. She obviously still had a little crush on him, even though she had no idea who he was anymore. It was a shallow infatuation left over from her girlhood. But the thought of bringing her even the slightest pain terrified him.

If his plan to move back to Sweetheart worked out, he would tread carefully and draw the boundary lines. Perhaps he could help her find the right husband. It was shocking she wasn't already married. Her silky blonde hair and soft blue eyes would catch the attention of any man. She'd probably broken a few hearts. More than a few, if that cocky cowboy from the reunion was any indication. Evan should find her someone better.

He placed a finger on top of her menu and pushed it down until her face was visible. "Are you afraid our little kiss will get around to Boone?"

"Boone?" Her brow wrinkled. "Why would I care what he thinks?"

"Don't you have a date with him this Friday?"

"How do you know that?" She lowered the menu to the table.

"He mentioned it at the reunion. If you're dating Boone, why does the whole town assume we're engaged?"

A young college-aged waitress with a streak of purple in her short, choppy hair approached. She spoke around a mouthful of chewing gum. "Are y'all ready?"

They both ordered the lunch special and waited until the girl was out of earshot before continuing the conversation.

"I'm not 'dating' Boone." Deanna made air quotes. "We've gone out a few times for fun. Nothing official."

"Does he wish it were otherwise?"

Pink tinged her cheeks. "Why, Evan Colter, are you jealous?"

"What?" He shifted, and the vinyl bench squeaked beneath him. "Of course not. But I feel a sense of responsibility for you since we grew up together."

"Boone and I grew up together too." Amusement filled her voice. "I'm sure he'd love to take responsibility for me, but I'd never let him. Poor thing. I've told him more than once it won't work, but he refuses to give up."

"Then why keep dating him?"

Deanna shrugged. "Weekends get lonely sitting around the house."

Evan knew all about lonely weekends. He usually spent them in his sweats on the couch, watching football and napping. He'd once been the life of the party, but his mindless search for happiness left him bitter and jaded. Nothing satisfied him for long. No shallow entertainment compared to the joy he'd felt as a boy. When he had a home. And a family that stretched far beyond his actual blood relations. Now that he'd stepped onto that cherished land, he didn't want to leave. How could he go back to the big city and the empty days?

Deanna's energetic voice interrupted the downward trajectory of his mood. "Once you move back, I'll have plenty to keep me busy. It's going to take a ton of elbow grease and loving care to renovate the ranch. The sooner we get started, the better."

"We?" He smiled at her.

"You don't think I'd make you tackle that project alone, do you? We need to get started yesterday."

"There's still the little problem of someone else owning the place. And even if Mrs. Hammington agrees, it will take a while to move her out. Who knows when I'd actually move in? I may have to stay in Dallas until things are finalized. I can't afford to live at the B&B for months."

"I have a great idea!"

He met her sparkling regard. "What's that?"

"Stay at my place."

"What?" He shifted. The bench squeaked again. It was getting to be a habit. "I can't stay with you. We're not actually en—" He looked over his shoulder at the other diners and lowered his voice. "We're not really engaged."

"What on earth are you implying, Evan Colter?" Deanna crossed her arms. "What kind of woman do you think I am?

Even if we were engaged, I wouldn't let you stay with me alone. I still live with my mother in the same house you used to eat dinner at as a kid."

"Oh." He let out an exaggerated breath and relaxed.

"You don't have to seem so relieved." She sniffed. "A girl could get offended. But I'm sure Mama would be fine with you using the guest room for a few days. It will give you a chance to get reacquainted with Sweetheart and set things right with Mrs. Hammington." She uncrossed her arms and bounced on the bench. "If things go well, you could drive to Dallas and pack your stuff right away."

He shook his head. "Do you always do things at this breakneck pace?"

The sparkle in her eyes intensified. "Only when it's something I'm interested in."

He didn't miss the subtext. "I don't know …"

"Just consider it. Don't worry. I'll keep my hands to myself." She gave him a saucy wink. "For now."

Chapter Ten

Deanna sank into a dented cushion on Mrs. Hammington's frayed plaid couch. Despite her best efforts urging Evan to stay at her house, he'd chosen to spend another night at the bed-and-breakfast. They'd promised to meet at the ranch in the morning to set the record straight on their so-called engagement, but she'd beaten him there, and Mrs. Hammington had refused to let her wait on the porch.

The older woman raised the foot of her well-worn recliner. It popped up with a rusty clang. "Where's that handsome fiancé of yours?"

Deanna twisted the ends of the pink chiffon scarf holding her hair. "Mrs. Hammington, I have a confession to make."

The old woman's sharp gaze took her in. "Does it have something to do with this out-of-the-blue engagement of yours?"

Deanna cast a glance out the window, wishing with all her might that Evan would arrive and interrupt this awkward moment. But the long gravel driveway was empty. "I'm afraid I've leaped before I looked again. I thought you'd enjoy living in town, I wanted Evan to move back to Sweetheart and build his boys' ranch, and I got carried away because I—"

"Stop right there." Mrs. H held up her hand. "I don't want to know the rest."

"But you don't understand. I'm not—"

"Is something wrong with your hearing, girlie? I said, 'I don't want to know.'" She relaxed in her easy chair. "Answer me one question. Do you want to be Mrs. Evan Colter?"

"More than anything in the world."

"Then that's good enough for me. You go ahead and make that dream happen. I'll be rootin' for you. And save me a front seat at the wedding."

Wedding? From her mouth to God's ears. But that day was a long way off, if it ever even happened. Deanna waged a silent war with her conscience. She'd promised Evan she would set things right, but Mrs. Hammington wasn't cooperating. Couldn't Deanna just go along with the lovely woman's story?

No. A promise was a promise.

She tried again. "Are you saying you understand—"

A knock sounded.

"Perfect timing." Mrs. Hammington chuckled, lowered the foot of the recliner, and rose. "Let's go see who it is."

They made their way to the front door and opened it.

A guilty Evan stood on the other side. He rubbed his bearded cheek. "Did you tell her, Dee?"

"I tried, but she—"

"I'm glad you're here, Evan." Mrs. H interrupted. "I've already called the banker about the sale. He made an appointment for us tomorrow at noon. You can drive me." She urged Deanna out of the house. "Take your fiancée with you, and let me get some rest. You two always visit during my naptime."

"Mrs. Hammington,"—Evan put his foot over the threshold—"that's what we want to talk about. Dee isn't—"

"I haven't got the energy for Hurricane Deanna today." The old woman yawned and pushed on the door.

Evan yanked his foot back as the door slammed in their faces. He stalked off the porch, stopped in the front yard, and leveled accusing eyes at Deanna.

She hurried to join him and held up both palms. "I tried to tell her. I swear. But she kept cutting me off. Still, I think—"

"This is insane." He ran both hands through his hair and grasped the ends. "I can't let her sell me the ranch under false pretenses."

Deanna took hold of his hands and drew them away from his head. "She asked you to drive her tomorrow, right? Once she's in the truck, you can lock the doors and make her listen to the truth."

He looked encouraged by the suggestion. Deanna stared at the strong fingers clasped within hers. Mrs. Hammington already seemed wise to them. The confession probably wasn't necessary, but it would put Evan more at ease. Unless the cagey old woman chose to cut him off as she had Deanna.

His hands tightened around hers as he surveyed the ranch. "I love this place. If I come back here, I might remember what it's like to feel happy again."

"Then do it." Deanna swiveled in front of him. "Come back. Be happy. I've told you before. Mrs. H wants to sell this place. You're doing her a favor."

"Things got so twisted with the whole engagement rumor." His fingers twitched as if he wanted to grab his hair again. "I hate lies. They disgust me to my very core."

"Then let's make it the truth." Deanna took a step closer until only a few inches separated their bodies. "Let's get married."

Chapter Eleven

E van blinked. And blinked again. He must have heard her wrong. When they were little kids, Dee used to declare emphatically how they were going to get married someday. But they weren't six years old anymore.

"Excuse me?"

"Don't freak out." Deanna laughed. "I'm not suggesting we call Pastor Thibodeaux and book a wedding date. But Mrs. Hammington has agreed to sell you the ranch because she thinks we're getting married. The whole town thinks it. Just goes to show how gossip spreads faster than a virus. If we let them keep thinking we're engaged awhile, it might make it easier for you."

"Easier?"

Deanna started to speak, but paused. Her soft fingers stroked his wrist. "I know it must be hard coming back. Seeing people. Hearing the whispers. But you don't have to face it alone. I'll be your bodyguard."

He perused her petite frame and smirked. "I doubt a runt like you can do much damage."

Her lips turned down in an exaggerated scowl. "Don't

count me out because I'm short. I took judo lessons while you were gone. I bet I could knock you off your feet if I wanted to." She released his hands and wrapped her arms tight around his waist. "This is your home, Evan. It's where you belong. And I intend to make sure you stay here."

He snorted. "How? Are you going to use some of those judo moves on me?"

"Anything it takes." Deanna squeezed him tighter, staring up at him with eyes wide open. "Come home, Evan Colter."

A strong Texas breeze hit his back, knocking him off-kilter. He staggered to the side and held on to Deanna. That's what life had been like for so long—everything out of balance. He ached for home. And not just Sweetheart. Yes, he'd longed for the town, but what he'd truly missed was much more. He missed the person he was when Sweetheart was home, before he discovered what a weak man his father was and how many people his selfishness had hurt.

He took in the family ranch. It looked the same as always, except a little worse for wear. He could fix the rundown surface problems. But even though Evan had returned to the place where he was the happiest, it didn't feel the same.

Perhaps he'd hoped a magical inner healing would generate in his soul when he drove onto the property. But it hadn't happened. His crusty heart still sported the scars from his past. Would he ever feel at home again? Had the whole world been tainted by the death of his innocence and the revelation that the world wasn't good? That *God* wasn't good.

Everything was different now.

The breeze blew a lock of Deanna's hair against his chest, reminding him of her presence.

"I don't know where to start," he whispered.

"I'll tell you where." She leaned far enough back that he

could see her face. "Start at 1401 Crepe Myrtle Lane. That's my address, in case you've forgotten."

"I rode my bike to your house more times than I can count." He stepped out of her embrace. "I remember where you live."

"Great. After you and Mrs. Hammington finalize the paperwork on the ranch tomorrow, you can drive to Dallas and shove all your stuff in a trailer."

Evan buried his hands in his pockets. "I rent a furnished apartment, and I don't have many keepsakes." He wasn't sure if it was because he wasn't the sentimental type or if he hadn't created any memories in the last twenty years he wanted to hold on to. "I doubt I'll need a trailer. My truck bed can easily hold my belongings with room to spare."

"Uh-oh. I'm a closet hoarder. That may make it difficult for us when we set up housekeeping." Deanna poked him in the stomach with a teasing finger. "Just kidding." She looped her arm around his and towed him toward the truck. "However much or little you own, throw it in a box and head to Sweetheart as quick as you can. Then we can get started restoring the Double Heart Ranch to her former glory."

"We?" he halted.

"Of course." She flashed a butter-wouldn't-melt smile at him. "I can't have the town thinking I'm a terrible fiancée." Deanna released him, sashayed to her bicycle, and patted the seat. "Be a darling and load this in your truck. It will save me the long pedal to town." Once she popped the handle on the passenger side, she climbed into the cab and shut the door.

Evan stood where she'd left him, dizzy from the aftereffects of Hurricane Deanna. Had he agreed to the fake engagement thing? He couldn't recall the exact details. Apparently, he'd also agreed to move back to Sweetheart since he'd already talked about packing up the truck. And he might even be staying at Deanna's house.

He scratched the top of his head. Was it really less than forty-eight hours since he'd walked into the reunion? How could his life be flipped on its head so fast?

Evan harbored a sneaking suspicion it had less to do with his desire to purchase the old homestead and everything to do with Deanna Day.

Chapter Twelve

S trains of subtle instrumental music played from the dining room speakers of the Rare Ribeye as customers enjoyed the ritzy atmosphere of Sweetheart's most expensive steakhouse. There wasn't a crying baby to be found in the Friday night crowd. Between the tables, staff moved like silent ninjas, appearing in an instant to refill water glasses or retrieve a fork that dropped on the carpet.

Deanna's plate was a gourmet masterpiece with an artful slash of sauce surrounding the filet mignon. Her knife slid through the meat with the slightest effort. She cut an elegant-sized bite, placed it in her mouth, and moaned. "Oh my word. This is the best steak I've had in years."

Boone grinned at her from across the table. "That's because you've never tried my T-bone Extraordinaire. Next time, I'll grill you a feast that'll put this one to shame."

Next time?

Instead of answering, Deanna took a second bite. She'd only kept this date with Boone to break the bad news. There would be no more dates. Ever.

The peppery juice from the meat barely registered as she

chewed. What was the kindest way to tell him? Should she rip the Band-Aid off and get it over with? After all, she'd tried to discourage him in the past, but the dogged cowboy kept reappearing.

Boone sat in ironed jeans, a dark-blue dress shirt, and a bolo tie. He'd even taken his hat off.

Deanna set down her silverware and folded her hands on the table. "Listen, Boone—"

"I'm mighty glad Evan Colter beat it to Dallas, where he belongs." Boone slathered a dollop of butter on a piece of bread. "You can't imagine the wacky rumors swirlin' around town. Everyone's saying you're gonna marry him and move out to the old Colter ranch. What kind of lamebrain puts these crazy ideas in people's heads? They'll realize the truth now that he's gone."

"But he's coming back."

"You sure about that?"

Deanna's shoulders tensed. Truth be told, she wasn't sure. She hoped he was coming back, but hadn't talked to him in four days. As far as she knew, he'd visited the bank with Mrs. Hammington and then left town without a word. What if they hadn't worked out a deal? What if he'd confessed everything to Mrs. H and she'd refused to sell?

What if he didn't return?

Her fingers clenched atop the fine linen tablecloth. He had to come back. God wouldn't be so cruel as to bring him to town for two days and then take him away again.

She drank her sweet tea before answering. "Boone, there's something important you should know. Those crazy rumors you mentioned began with me. I plan to marry Evan Colter."

Her date choked on the huge bite of steak he'd put in his mouth. His neck reddened. Boone pounded on his chest and gasped. "Have you gone loco? He won't marry you."

"Why not?" Deanna managed to keep her voice polite, but she felt like tossing a dinner roll at the idiot's face.

"Listen, Deanna." Boone hacked and took a swig of his water. "I don't know what that shyster promised, but you can't trust him."

"Careful, Boone." Ice entered her tone.

"You're too sweet and naïve to suspect people of things, but Evan Colter isn't the boy you knew. Don't forget, his father was a con man. I bet he's a chip off the old block."

"The block you need to worry about is the one you wear under your oversized cowboy hat." Deanna tossed her napkin onto the table. Her chair legs grated against the floor as she stood. She planted both fists on the table and leaned forward. "If you ever dare talk about my fiancé like that again, I'll demonstrate why I was the first person in my judo class to earn a black belt."

After grabbing her vintage red pillbox purse, she stalked through the crowded dining room while ignoring the stares of the other patrons. Deanna passed the hostess station, thrust the front door open, stomped onto the sidewalk, and halted. She glanced at the parking lot, where Boone's crew cab truck with monster wheels waited. There was no way she would ask him for a ride. She tapped her toe against the pavement. Her kitten heels weren't the best choice of footwear for the occasion. But how was she supposed to guess she'd be walking home?

Deanna raised her chin. "Might as well get started."

She walked down Hidalgo Boulevard and took a right onto Main Street. If she kept this pace, it should take fifteen to twenty minutes to reach home. Her tummy grumbled. Two bites of steak hadn't been nearly enough. She observed Rosa's Taqueria on the other side of the road and paused. Perhaps she'd eat lunch first. Even find someone to give her a ride home. Her spirits lifted. She skipped across the street and entered the restaurant.

Deanna scanned the taqueria. It was lunchtime, and not a single table was available. There was one empty seat in the whole place. In the corner, Renae Smith sat at a small two-seater by herself, finishing a plate of enchiladas. At five-foot-ten, she was hard to miss. Her bleached blonde hair was teased in a poofy swirl reminiscent of the eighties. A jumble of miscellaneous silver jewelry hung from her throat and cascaded into the low-cut neckline of her T-shirt.

Deanna hesitated.

They'd never been close, even in school. The woman's interests ran more toward the wild side of things. She'd even been mixed up with a guy who went to prison.

But Deanna was hungry.

She crossed to the tiny table and plopped onto the empty seat. "Hey, Renae. We haven't talked in a while."

The blonde eyed her. "Yeah, it's been forever. Literally."

Deanna nodded. "Okay. I admit it. I'm starving, and this is the only empty seat. But that doesn't mean we can't get to know each other better. You're one of the few single women around my age left in town. We should form a club."

A sarcastic burst of air left Renae's lips. "What would we call it, Spinsters Anonymous?"

Deanna cringed. "I was thinking more along the lines of Sweetheart's Sassy Single Ladies. We're not far gone enough to be considered spinsters."

"Maybe *you're* not." Renae folded her arms on the table. "Don't you have something going on with Evan Colter? Word has it, you won't be single for much longer."

"Oh,"—Deanna rubbed her brow—"right."

"He's rocking the mountain man look these days. I always did favor 'em rugged." She tittered. "But that's not your style.

You dress like the women in the fifties who wore their pearl necklaces to vacuum. Does the flannel bother you?"

Deanna tilted her head. "Truth be told, I hadn't considered it. Whatever he wears is all right with me." *As long as he stays where I can see him.*

"What about the beard?" Renae turned her head a little to the right and arched a well-constructed brow. "Does it scratch when he kisses you?"

The tiny peck they'd shared in the diner had hardly given her time to process the details. What would it be like to really kiss Evan Colter? And would she ever get the chance?

Deanna sighed. "Honestly, I didn't notice one way or the other."

Renae scrunched her face. "Then, girl, you must not be doing it right."

"Doing what right?" A deep voice asked behind them.

Deanna spun on her chair to find Evan. He wore jeans, a black shirt, and a light-brown jacket. To her, it looked better than a tuxedo. Had he heard what they were talking about?

Who cared?

"Evan!" She sprang to her feet and wrapped her arms around his neck. "When did you get back in town?"

He stumbled to the side, righted them both, and gave her shoulder an awkward pat before stepping away. "Just now. I thought I'd have lunch before driving to your house."

Renae pushed her plate away. "That's my cue to beat it."

"Don't be silly," Deanna said. "We three can eat together."

The woman's bright red lips twisted. "No thanks. I've got to pick up my nephew from school. Besides, it sounds like you two need all the practice you can get."

"Practice?" Evan lifted his brows.

"Don't mind us." Deanna smoothed the sides of her hair. "We were having some girl talk."

"Y'all be good now." Renae winked at Deanna as she scooted between them.

Evan settled into the vacated chair. The waitress came to take their orders and cleared away Renae's leftovers.

Deanna sat, propped her elbows on the table, and rested her chin on her palm. "I'm thrilled to see you. Honestly, I wasn't sure you were coming back."

"I'd better come back. The bank is drafting a mortgage with my name on it."

"Mrs. H agreed to sell you the property? What happened?"

"That day we went to the bank together, we finalized the specifics. All that's left is the signing. I'm supposed to meet her there in an hour. Her sister is dropping her off."

"Did you"—she looked around and lowered her voice—"did you tell her the truth? About us, I mean."

Evan shook his head. "I tried, but every time I broached the subject, she'd cut me off. I flat-out said she had you and me wrong, but before I finished explaining, she said she didn't want to know, that she was happy thinking what she was thinking, and if anything was different than what she was thinking, I should keep it to myself." He scratched his head. "Or something along those lines. By that time, I was so confused, I wasn't sure what to say."

Deanna laughed. "Mrs. H is a savvy lady. You can be sure she's got our number."

"One thing I was sure of, she was happy to sell the ranch to me. I saw the relief on her face when she admitted the place was too huge for her to keep up with anymore. She plans to stay with her sister in town for the time being."

"We'd better get out there and help her pack her treasures."

The waitress arrived with two heaping plates of food. Deanna clapped at the sight of the giant huarache. The soft bread with the crispy fried coating was piled high with lettuce, cheese, beans, diced chicken, and guacamole.

"Oh my word, I'm famished." She cut a corner off the huarache, picked it up with her fingers, and raised it to her mouth.

Evan grabbed his fork. "Why are you eating late?"

Deanna paused midbite. Should she mention her date with Boone? It's not like Evan and she were truly engaged. But somehow, it felt dishonest to hide it. Wouldn't it be better to get it all out in the open?

"I ... I was having lunch with Boone Richardson."

She took a giant bite to prevent follow-up questions, but Evan didn't ask any. He pursed his lips, nodded, and added a dash of hot sauce to his tacos.

Humph. Would it kill him to be a tiny bit jealous that she was eating with another man? Instead, he finished his first taco in three bites without spilling a drop on his clothes or his beard. Deanna zeroed in on the chin hair. Would it scratch if he ever gave her a decent kiss? It appeared soft. Silky even.

"What are you staring at?"

"Huh?" She met his gaze. "I-I—nothing. I was ... wondering ... about your beard."

"My beard?" He ran his fingers over his jaw. "What about it?"

"Does it, I mean, do you—do you ever get food caught in it?"

What a lame question. No wonder he was looking at her like she just fell off the turnip truck.

Deanna took a drink from her water glass and fanned herself with a paper napkin. "Rosa needs to crank up the air in here."

"No." Evan's mouth quirked to one side. "I don't get food caught in my beard. What's the matter? You don't like it?"

"It's not that." Deanna laid the napkin on the table and smoothed it with nervous fingers. "Although I'm not normally a fan of facial hair, on you it works." Maybe a joke would alleviate the awkwardness. "Of course, I'll expect you to shave for the wedding."

Evan closed his eyes, and an exasperated laugh escaped him. "You are completely nuts." His smile disappeared, and he peered at her. "Sorry. I should watch what I say."

"Why? I *am* nuts. Everyone in town knows it."

He smiled again. "Yeah, but we haven't exactly been close in the last few decades. Yet, I keep finding myself acting as if we're a couple of kids riding our bikes around town."

"I *still* ride my bike around town, at least until you give me those driving lessons. And I'm perfectly fine with picking up our relationship where we left off. You can joke all you want" —her lips curled in a grin—"and I'll keep saying I want to marry you when I grow up. Since I obviously still have a ways to go."

Evan took a bite of his second taco without bothering to correct her. He swallowed before speaking. "Does your mom know you offered to help me renovate the ranch?"

"I told her. When you stay with us, she plans to bake you a fresh batch of oatmeal raisin cookies."

"No, thanks." He took a drink of his ice water. "I've already checked into the B&B again. I'll bunk there until I move out to the ranch."

Deanna huffed. "Fine. Waste your money on a hotel bill. But at least come by for lunch after church on Sunday."

"I don't go to church anymore."

"Since when?

"Since I stopped believing God was on my side."

His statement floored her. The Evan of her youth had always been the sweetest, most sincere believer she knew. But now, his matter-of-fact denial of God's goodness sounded ten times worse than if he'd ranted and raved. She watched him eat, an ache like heartburn in her chest. He'd suffered so much on his own. Could she help him find his way home in more ways than one?

Deanna sipped her sweet tea. "You know that will need to change before the wedding, right? I want the father of my children to set a good example."

He finished the second taco and mimicked her cheerful tone. "You know we're not really getting married, right?"

"We'll see."

"Pffft." He rolled his eyes at her and grabbed his final taco.

Deanna's smile was confident, but a prickle of fear danced under her skin. A multitude of things stood in the way of a real relationship with Evan. She knew he still saw her as a bratty little sister. Their engagement was a joke, a misunderstanding they'd have to confess to the gossips when the time came. Unless she won his heart for real. If, by some miracle, he ever did fall for her, would he change his mind if he found out her long-buried secret? Or would he climb in his truck and drive as fast and as far away as possible?

Chapter Thirteen

Evan opened the bank door for Mrs. Hammington. She took slow, careful steps down the concrete stairs and squinted at the afternoon sun. It glowed rather than blazed. A cool autumn breeze brought a welcome relief from the humidity that had hung on Sweetheart since his arrival.

He held up a manila envelope. "Thank you, Mrs. H. It must have been a hard decision for you to sell, but it means a lot to me."

The stoic woman sniffed. "No thanks necessary for doing what was logical. I can't manage that big ol' place anymore." She looked past him and smirked. "And I'm guessing you two will put all the room to good use."

"Two?" He jumped when a dainty hand patted his back.

"Is it settled?" Deanna's beaming face swerved around his arm. "Have the papers been signed?"

"It's official. I'm homeless," Mrs. Hammington deadpanned.

"Oh, stop." Deanna swatted her lightly. "Your sister is delighted you'll be living with her. She's been lonely since her husband passed away."

"I know the feeling." Mrs. H sighed. "Days are endless when there's only one of you." She poked Deanna. "That's why y'all should get a move on. Life's more fun when you share it."

Evan shook his head. "Mrs. Hammington, we've tried to tell you. We're not—"

"Never you mind." Mrs. H pouted. "Just let an old woman think what makes her happy."

"Evan Colter!" A new voice bellowed.

Everyone turned to the opposite side of Main Street. Lanette Johnson stood in front of the manicure shop. Her short, stylish blonde hair, along with her rhinestone-studded jean jacket, matching pants, and red patent leather heels, gleamed in the sunlight. She hustled across the road with a speed that belied her sixty-plus years. Once she reached their small group, she skidded to a stop, fingers pressed to her heaving bosom. "Is it really you, son?"

Her voice was the same as he remembered, confident and a little louder than the acceptable volume.

"Hello, Mrs. Johnson." His lips formed a tight line that was the best imitation of a smile he could muster.

"Mrs. Johnson? Forget the formalities, sugar. Call me Aunt Lanette, like when you were a boy."

"I'm not a boy anymore."

Tension sizzled in the air.

Deanna shifted in front of him. "Hi, Aunt Lanette. Guess what?" She gave her a quick hug. "Mrs. Hammington decided to sell the Double Heart Ranch to Evan, and they signed the paperwork today."

"I heard." Lanette studied Evan and Deanna. "In fact, there've been quite a lot of interesting rumors flying lately."

Evan's shoulders tightened. Was Lanette Johnson trying to start a fight?

She waggled a finger at Deanna. "I checked with our girl

here to make sure I wasn't missing any wedding plans, but she told me not to listen to the gossipmongers. How long before it's official? Am I going to have one foot in the grave before I see you married?"

Mrs. Hammington cackled. "Not if Deanna has anything to say about it."

Deanna tugged at the lace collar of her blouse. "Please, y'all. You'll scare Evan away."

"Marjorie, did you finally sell the ranch?" Lanette raised her thinly plucked eyebrows at Mrs. Hammington. "It's high time you stopped hiding out there in the wild. It will be good to have you in town. When are you moving your stuff?"

Mrs. H jerked her head to Evan and Deanna. "The young'uns offered to help me, so we'll get started tomorrow. I'm sure Evan wants to stop living out of a suitcase."

"Don't worry about me," he said. "You can take your time. I'm okay where I am."

"And where is that?" asked Lanette.

"The bed-and-breakfast on Bluebell Street." He spoke without looking at her and turned his body to face Mrs. Hammington, effectively blocking Mrs. Johnson from his vision. He knew it was petty, but a visceral reaction welled inside of him at the sight of the woman. His father had been arrested because of her and her husband, Harry. They were the ones who led the charge to oust his dad from public office. "Come on, Mrs. H. I'll drive you home." He took the older woman by the elbow.

"What about Deanna?" Mrs. Hammington dug in her heels. "I'm sure she'd like to spend time with you. Why not take her to lunch? Lanette will give me a ride, won't you?" She motioned to the other woman.

"That's not a bad idea, Marjorie. We'll let these two enjoy their youth. You and I both know how fast it's gone."

"Speak for yourself." Mrs. Hammington sniffed. "I plan to outlive Methuselah."

Lanette moved into his field of vision once again. "If you get tired of the B&B, Evan, you're always welcome at my house. We'd love to have you." She withdrew a business card from her purse and held it out. "Here's my phone number."

He made no move to take it.

Lanette quirked a brow and slipped the card in his jacket pocket. "Come on, Marjorie." She looped an arm around Mrs. Hammington, and they walked away.

Evan released a slow breath, but it didn't do much good. A tight sensation gripped his chest like a steel vise squeezing his heart. Usually, the emotions he felt when reminiscing about the past were sadness and shame, but every once in a while, a long-buried fury resurrected.

How could Lanette Johnson invite him to her house as if her husband and she hadn't sat in a courtroom and testified against their lifelong friend? Evan's father had committed the crimes they accused him of. He deserved punishment. But still.

Deanna's hip bumped his. "Are you okay?"

"Fine."

"You don't look fine."

"I didn't realize you were a psychologist. How do I look, doctor?" His words scraped out like sandpaper.

Deanna blinked. Her usual sunny expression disappeared, replaced by a puckered brow. "Forget it. I shouldn't have pushed you. I know we just ate, but I'm still hungry. Let's go get dessert at Patty's Pizza Place." She whirled so fast her wide skirt swirled, revealing a poofy pink slip underneath. Her flat, dressy shoes clicked against the pavement as she retreated.

Evan rubbed a hand against his beard. Why had he baited the one person in the world who was still on his side?

"Wait up." He hurried to follow Deanna. "I'm sorry, Dee. I didn't mean to—to shut you out. I'm just ..."

Her face was a polite mask, eyes a little too wide and small smile a little too tight.

He wasn't sure how to finish his sentence. He was just what? A jerk? Most definitely. But he'd already said he was sorry, so how else could he fix the tense atmosphere? Another apology? Change the subject? Distract her?

Evan cleared his throat. "So when's my party?"

Deanna's steps slowed. "Your what?"

"My welcome home party. You promised me one."

"I did?" She stopped. "When?"

"Hmm." He wrinkled his forehead in an exaggerated display of thinking. "Not sure. Was it about eighteen years ago?"

"Excuse me?" She laughed.

"When I was living in Dallas, you wrote me a letter asking me to come back to Sweetheart. And you promised to throw the biggest party anyone had ever seen if I did."

"Wait a minute." Deanna held up a hand. "Are you talking about the letter I wrote you in tenth grade? I didn't know you got it."

"My cousin Rex gave it to me when he came for a visit. He said you threatened him within an inch of his life if he didn't deliver it."

"Rex told me he'd done as instructed, but I wasn't sure if he was telling the truth or too scared to admit he threw it away." She grabbed his arm. "You really got my letter?"

"Yep. What you wrote made an impression. Every now and then, I'd consider taking you up on your offer. But I lacked the courage. Until one day, I visited *The Sweetheart Clarion*'s website on a whim, saw a story about Mrs. Beauregard's retirement party, and hoped perhaps enough time had passed.

It prodded me into contacting Mrs. H to ask about the ranch. Even though she refused my offer to buy it, I sensed it wasn't a hard-and-fast no, which gave me the guts to attend Mrs. Beauregard's party. I hit the road and made it all the way to the elementary school parking lot before I chickened out when I tried to walk in the building."

"I was afraid you were going to drive away."

"I was. If you hadn't stopped me, I'd have probably retreated to Dallas without talking to anyone." He gave a sad smile. "But you kept your promise. You were waiting for me."

She bit her lip. "I'm sorry not everyone welcomed you that night."

"It's understandable. My dad hurt a lot of people. When you live in a town as small as ours, folks have long memories." He scratched the side of his neck. "But my memory needs some work because I forgot how to speak to a lady. Especially one who's only ever done me good."

Her gaze softened. "I'm trying to help."

"I know." He laid his free hand on top of the one still holding his arm. "Let's just say, meeting Lanette Johnson again got under my skin."

"But why? Aunt Lanette was happy to see you. She even offered to let you stay at her house."

"I'd rather not talk about it now. Someday."

Her indrawn breath told him she wanted to argue, to push him. Instead, Deanna closed her lips, curled them inward, and nodded. It must have taken a monumental effort for her to let it go.

Evan chucked her under the chin. "How about I pay for dessert? Let's go."

They walked in silence to the restaurant. Evan carried the envelope with the ranch's deed. What should've been a happy moment of celebrating the purchase was awkward and stilted thanks to Lanette. His fingers grasped the envelope tight. Would his new life in Sweetheart always be colored by the past? It wasn't merely the bad things like the Johnsons' betrayal. Even the good memories were painful because they highlighted how long it had been since he'd felt anything more than a surface level of happiness. Deep joy no longer existed in his life.

Was it gone forever? Did a person experience that kind of exhilaration and innocence in childhood because they were too young to know better? Or could he find the same happiness again?

They reached the pizza place, and Deanna spun to face him at the door.

"I'm warning you, Evan. I'm letting this go for your sake. But I plan to hold you to that 'someday' you mentioned. You've got to share the painful stuff to recover fully." She poked him in the chest. "And don't pull that men-don't-talk-about-their-feelings junk on me. You *are* going to heal inside, and you *are* going to get comfortable in Sweetheart again." She pointed at her torso. "And I *am* going to throw you the party I promised. Just you wait. It'll be a shindig for the town history books." Her skirt billowed again as she opened the door and entered the restaurant.

The vise around Evan's heart loosened at her words, and a sense of hope pervaded his soul. Maybe she was right. Maybe he could find relief from the ghosts that tortured him. If a spitfire like Deanna Day was on his side, anything was possible.

Chapter Fourteen

Deanna forced herself to maintain a composed gait as they left Patty's after eating two huge slices of cookie crumble pizza. What she wanted to do was dance down the sidewalk and hang off a lamppost like Gene Kelly. The very fact Evan hadn't rushed away after dessert proved he appreciated her company. Right?

Sweetheart's Main Street certainly resembled an old-fashioned movie musical set. Patriotic displays of red snapdragons, white pansies, and blue petunias filled the giant stone flower pots lining the road. Colorful, striped awnings decorated the storefronts. And a mix of cheerful oldies played from intermittent speakers.

"What are your plans for the rest of the day?" Deanna asked.

Evan shrugged. "There isn't much to do until I get Mrs. H moved off the ranch."

"Why don't you attend the town meeting tonight in the new city hall?"

"Where's that?"

"They renovated the old Sweetheart Memorial Bank. It

was Katherine's idea. You should see what they've done with the place. The main floor is a public assembly area with smaller conference rooms along the side. Then the second floor became offices for the clerk, city council, and m-mayor."

Stupid girl! Evan must have bad memories associated with any mayoral connections. Why had she brought up something that would make him think of his father?

Evan's face showed no reaction, good or bad. "What time is the meeting?"

"Huh? Oh. Seven o'clock. I'm in charge of refreshments, so I'll be there early."

They approached the Conroe Theatre, and Deanna paused. She stared at the scrolling carved masonry along the roof. The year 1915 was etched into the stone above the marquee. Even though the sign still lit with welcome messages for the town festivals when visitors flooded the quaint streets, Deanna knew it was a façade. What sat inside was a musty, decrepit auditorium filled with warped wooden folding seats, water stains streaking the ancient wallpaper, and holes in the floorboards of the stage.

In her youth, the community had used the historic building for special programs. She'd played Orphan #3 in a theater summer camp version of *Annie*. But structural issues forced the city to close down the theater. Now, Sweetheart's elementary school gym was used for any community productions. Through the years, she'd worked her way up from Orphan #3 to starring roles in most of the shows, but the minuscule stage in the school gymnasium sucked the romance from the scenes. They would be much better on a genuine stage like the one hidden inside the Conroe.

"What a waste," Deanna murmured.

Evan studied the theater. "Waste of what?"

"A waste of all that sawdust and atmosphere. Remember the good old days when we used to hold the shows here?"

He clasped his hands behind him. "Vaguely. Wasn't I the prince in Cinderella or something?"

"Rapunzel."

"Oh, right. I had to scale a ladder while pretending to climb Amarisa McFarland's fake braid and almost broke my neck."

"The price of fame. At least your name was highlighted on the playbill. Mine was on the last page in a long list of people singing in *The Chorus*."

Evan walked to the old box office and peered through the glass window. "What happened to this place?"

"It wore out, and no one wanted to fork over the money to fix it. I wish the town would renovate it like they did with the bank." Deanna wandered to the entrance and jiggled the decorative brass knob. One of the double doors popped open, and she gasped.

Evan held up both hands and backed away. "I can't afford any more criminal activity on my record."

"Oh, stop." She made a face at him. "Someone forgot to lock the door. We'll be doing the owner a favor by checking inside to make sure nothing was stolen."

"Uh-huh." Evan's right eyebrow arched. "You're doing it for the owner's sake."

"There's no harm in reliving a few old memories." Deanna looked both ways and sneaked inside. She poked her head out the door and motioned for him. "Come on, scaredy-cat."

He gave a long-suffering sigh, then followed her. With no windows in the lobby, it was hard to see anything. Deanna pulled out her cell phone and turned on its flashlight. The beam highlighted the frayed red carpet on the floor, empty poster boxes on the wall, and wooden planks with nails sticking out of them stacked in a side office.

The scent of mildew hung heavy in the air. Deanna held her breath as they traversed the small space and opened a door to the main auditorium. Her toe caught on a bulge in the carpet, and she tripped.

"Be careful." Evan took her by the elbow.

They walked down the aisle and drew near the front. The cell phone light illuminated a portion of the orchestra pit where the musicians had once sat.

Deanna's eyes filled with tears at the first sight of the empty stage beyond. "It's just like I remember it. I loved this theater so much. Did you know the Andrews Sisters performed here in the thirties? If only they had cell phone cameras back then." She sighed. "I always dreamed of standing in the middle of that same stage and singing a solo."

"Did you ever get the chance?"

"No. By the time I worked my way up to principal actor, they'd closed the theater. But I'm always the lead when we do the Sweet Shakes Weekend."

"Sweet Shakes Weekend? I don't remember that event."

"You'll soon get to see it in person. It began a few years ago." Deanna laughed. "We tacked it onto an idea Willy Walker hatched for a Shakespeare-themed cooking thing. He called it the Bard Barbecue. It started as a one-day cookout. But now it lasts a whole weekend, and visitors even drive in from out of town. Once people buy their food, they sit in the park and eat while we perform scenes from Shakespeare's plays on the gazebo stage."

"Sounds fun."

"It's a blast. You haven't lived 'til you've tasted Willy's Hamlet Ham Hocks. Or witnessed me play the death scene from *Romeo and Juliet*." Deanna extended an imaginary cup. "When the part came for me to grab the goblet of poison and find it empty, the prop manager had gotten confused and filled it to the brim. I got a face full of water." She feigned a coughing fit. "I proceeded to ad-lib a whole section explaining how the poison wasn't quick enough for my taste, and I must meet Romeo in Heaven sooner, before I grabbed the dagger. The locals laughed about it for weeks afterward. I've been waiting a whole year to get a second chance at that scene. This time, we'll get it right."

"Who's playing Romeo?"

"Boone Richardson."

Was it her imagination, or did Evan stiffen?

He left her side and peered into the orchestra pit. "What a mess. Looks like someone's been sneaking in here for a secret smoke break. There are cigarette butts everywhere."

"What?" Deanna hurried to check. She pointed her light at the floor. Tiny golden stubs littered the whole pit. "How dare they smoke in here? What if something caught fire? This beautiful, historic building might be damaged."

"Beautiful? Maybe only in your memory."

"Just because it's been through hard times doesn't mean it's not salvageable." Deanna spun in a circle, her light illuminating the spaces it passed. "There's a century of atmosphere packed in this building. With a little love and a lot of hard work, it could be restored to its former glory."

"Then why don't you do it?"

"Huh?" She pointed the light at him.

Evan squinted and pushed her hand down so the beam didn't hit him straight in the pupils. "If you love this theater, why don't you do something with it? Like they remodeled the bank into the city hall. From the way you talk, you thrive being on stage, and this would give you an outlet for all of your"—he smirked—"dramatic tendencies."

Deanna looped a strand of hair behind her ear. "Don't think the idea hasn't occurred to me."

"What's stopping you? Is it a money thing?"

"No. I live at home, don't own a car, and have very few expenses." She twirled, and her swing skirt flared. "Apart from stocking my closet with fabulous vintage dresses, that is. My credit is great, and I bet the town would cut me a sweet deal to have one less building empty on Main Street. But I doubt I could run the museum *and* renovate the theater."

"Hire someone else to run the museum. Your mom will understand."

"I know." She fussed with the buckle on her belt. "But it might make things hard on her. Ever since my dad passed away, change is scary for her, and I'd hate to put her through any unnecessary grief."

Did she sound cowardly? Her life had been in a holding pattern for so long. She wasn't sure if she was waiting for God's timing or if that was a convenient excuse because she was afraid to take the leap.

Any leap.

EVAN STUDIED THE BARELY LIT FACE IN FRONT OF HIM. IT WAS HARD TO read Deanna's expression in the semidarkness, but he sensed her unease. Who was he to make her uncomfortable? Changing the subject was a better idea.

"Makes sense." After taking hold of her shoulders, he pointed her toward the stage. "How about giving me a preview of Deanna Day singing a solo to the audience?"

"Oh, no. My voice isn't warmed up."

"Come on." He prodded her with a gentle elbow. "I bet you could give those Adams Sisters a run for their money."

"*Andrews* Sisters." She giggled. "Okay, you talked me into it.

Can you use your phone to point a light over by the stairs? I need both hands free if I'm going to give it my all."

He took his cell out and did as she suggested, making a well-lit path for her as she carefully made her way on stage.

Standing in the center, Deanna put her own phone away in a hidden pocket of her skirt, adjusted the folds, and trilled. *"Old MacDonald had a farm. E-I-E-I-O. And on that farm, he had a chick. E-I-E-I-O."* She folded her arms like wings and flapped them. *"With a cluck-cluck here. And a cluck-cluck there."* She poked her neck out like a chicken pecking the ground. *"Here a cluck. There a cluck. Everywhere a cluck-cluck."*

Evan tamped down the urge to laugh. "I take it back. That sister group has nothing to worry about."

"Meanie." Deanna stuck her tongue out at him.

"What about a classic song from when your clothes were in fashion?"

Her playful expression faded, and a soft look replaced it. "Irving Berlin composed a tune I used to play in my piano lessons."

"Irving?"

Deanna propped her fists on her hips. "Don't make fun of Mr. Berlin. He's the one who wrote 'God Bless America.'"

"My apologies, Mr. Berlin." Evan opened the Camera app without telling Deanna and hit Record. If she was about to lay her rendition of "I'm a Little Teapot" on him, he wanted to be ready. It would make great blackmail material. "Okay," he said. "Shoot."

Deanna took a deep breath and paused. Her voice came out tremulous at first, and she stared at the floorboards. *"Everything went wrong, and the whole day long, I'd feel so blue. For the longest while I'd forget to smile"*—she raised her chin and looked straight at him—*"then I met you."*

Evan stopped focusing on the screen. He gave Deanna his

full attention. Her voice grew strong and confident. The high, lilting sound echoed through the spacious room like a lone, cheerful birdsong as the sun rose in the huge Texas sky.

She kept singing. *"Now that my blue days have passed, now that I've found you at last"*—her grin was positively impish—*"I'll be loving you always with a love that's true always. When the things you've planned need a helping hand, I will understand always. Always."*

Evan shook his head. He didn't know if she was shameless or oozing self-confidence. But she could definitely carry a tune.

The one-woman show did a simple tap routine to the side. *"Days may not be fair always."* She tapped to the opposite side of the stage, careful to avoid holes in the flooring. *"That's when I'll be there always."* Returning to center stage, she stretched out her arms as if she were calling him with a siren song. *"Not for just an hour, not for just a day, not for just a year"*—she slowly lowered her hands, her eyes still reaching out for him—*"but always."*

The last echo faded, and something shifted in the room. Evan swallowed. For the first time in the years-long list of confessions by Deanna, his heart trembled. Her gaze fastened to his, drawing him in and refusing to let go.

His phone lowered, and he remembered the video was still recording. It broke him from the tug-of-war Deanna's eyes were playing with his soul. Evan fussed with his cell while she left the stage and descended to the ground floor.

She approached him with a different expression than her normal cheeky unconcern. A vulnerability shone on her face. "How did you like it?"

"I—" He pretended to mess with his phone to buy a little time. "It's a nice song, Dee."

"Thank you." Disappointment colored her tone. "We'd better get going before someone catches us."

She turned toward the door, but he stopped her.

"You should consider it. Buying the place, I mean." He gestured to the stage. "You seem comfortable up there. It's where you're meant to be."

"Do you really believe I could do it?"

Evan spread his hands in frustration. "Deanna Day, I believe there isn't anything in this world that can stop you if you set your mind to it."

"You think I'm that talented?"

"I think you're that stubborn."

Her laugh was musical, like the song she sang. It carried sweetness and light and hope for a better tomorrow.

"You're right. I *should* consider it, and I *am* that stubborn. About a lot of things." Deanna flicked a gentle finger under his chin. "Once I set my mind on something, I devote myself wholeheartedly."

Evan pretend-shuddered. "Is that a promise or a threat?"

Deanna sashayed to the exit without looking back. "Both."

He laughed under his breath. She was incorrigible, but he wouldn't have her any other way. In this sad world where so many people had let him down, it was nice to know one girl never changed.

Chapter Fifteen

"Does the town own the old theater on Main Street?" Deanna plopped onto the padded chair across from Katherine's desk.

"What?" Her friend's focus rose from the laptop screen. Piles of folders littered her desk. Her second-floor office faced the interior balcony that overlooked the lobby of the new city hall, where community events were held. A large glass window showed the marble tiles and carved wooden staircase leading to the ground floor. The lingering grandeur from days gone by put the mayor's utilitarian office to shame.

"Yes." Katherine clicked a key. "Why?"

Deanna twisted her fingers together on her lap. "I was just wondering ... I mean ... would it cost a lot ..." Was this crazy? Ideas for the theater had haunted her every moment after Evan and she parted ways.

Correction. Every moment that she wasn't dreaming about a certain gorgeous man with a golden beard. Her thoughts swung like a pendulum.

Theater. Evan. Theater. Evan.

Plans for shows and recitals and a vintage-themed

wedding venue to bring in extra income had flooded her mind. It all sounded feasible when she was by herself. But now the cold, hard facts were slapping her in the face.

"Helloooooo." Katherine waved in front of Deanna. "Why are you asking about the old theater, Dee?"

Deanna sucked in a lungful of air and jumped off the metaphorical cliff. "I want to buy it." She noted the way her friend's eyes bugged out like a goldfish and raced to explain. "I've always loved the Conroe. It's a dirty shame no one uses it anymore. Remember when we were kids and they used to hold shows there? If I buy it, our community theater company will have a decent stage to perform on."

"You want to buy it so you'll have a bigger place to act?"

"No! Well, yes. But it's not just about acting. I plan to renovate the entire building and rent it out. Town events, quinceañeras, weddings. There are truckloads of people online who are aching for unique, retro venues for their celebrations."

Katherine's left nostril wrinkled. "You haven't seen the inside lately. It would take serious work."

"About that"—Deanna cleared her throat—"Evan and I snuck in and did some exploring."

Her friend stood and hurried around the desk. "You and Evan?" She plopped on the empty chair beside Deanna. "How did that happen? Didn't he leave town?"

"He got back yesterday." Deanna swung her knees toward Katherine. "Mrs. Hammington sold him the old Double Heart Ranch. After he signed the papers, we were walking along Main Street past the Conroe. I tried one of the doors. It was open, so we poked around inside, and I started thinking how I'd love to buy—"

"Forget the theater." Katherine slashed a hand down. "We can talk about business later. How are things going with Evan? Have you made any progress?"

The right corner of Deanna's lips lifted in mischievous triumph. "Does smooching count? A few days ago, I kissed him in the diner in front of Mrs. Biddle."

"What!" Katherine flopped in her seat. "You kissed him already? Are you trying to make up for lost time?"

"Something like that."

"And how did he react?"

This part she didn't care to admit. Deanna shrugged a shoulder. "He didn't seem repulsed by it, but I wouldn't exactly call him swooning either. I get the feeling he was amused."

"Ouch." Katherine winced. "That must've stung."

"Not as much as not seeing him for twenty years. Besides, I'm used to Evan's indifference. And I'm not a kid anymore. If I have to serenade him with a love song onstage at the Conroe to get his attention, that's what I'll do."

"You might want to wait until he's warmed to the idea."

"Too late." Deanna grinned.

"You sang to him?" Katherine cocked her head. "How can you be so shameless?"

"You should talk. You went after Ryan like a bulldozer." She pointed at Katherine's baby bump. "It worked for y'all, didn't it?"

"Point taken." Katherine rubbed her belly. "So what's your next move?"

Deanna bit the inside of her lower lip. "I haven't got a clue. I need to make Evan acknowledge me as a woman instead of the annoying little sister who used to follow him around. Once that happens, I can finally admit ..."

"Admit what?"

"Never mind." Deanna didn't want to worry about the deeper issues now. Enough barriers stood between Evan and her without pondering the mistake she'd made two decades ago. Now that he was in town for good, there'd be time to fix things slowly.

Someone knocked on the door. It opened, and Betty Gannett, the town clerk, poked her head in. "Excuse me, Mayor Park. We're about to begin the staff meeting."

"Oh, right!" Katherine jumped up. "I'm sorry, Dee. We'll have to finish this later."

"Go." Deanna waved her off. "You're an important woman."

Her friend rolled her eyes. "Yes. The urgent matter we're discussing today is whether or not the Sweet Shakes Weekend should include a Renaissance-themed pet fashion show."

"What a great idea." Deanna stood. "You know what would make it even better? If there were a big stage like the Conroe's, where you could hold the event."

"Very subtle. I'll gather information on the theater and how much it's worth. Why don't you put together a proposal of all the ideas you told me? If you can convince the town council your renovation will bring new business to Sweetheart, I bet we can get them to make you a pretty good deal."

"Really?" Deanna threw her arms around Katherine. "I owe you big-time."

"Great. You can start by manning the refreshment table at the town meeting tonight. Make sure there are lots of cookies."

"Yes, ma'am." Deanna saluted. "Anything else?"

Katherine paused with her hand on the doorknob. "Just don't burst into song during the meeting."

She laughed. "If Evan's there, I can't promise anything. When he's around, it would take an Old Testament prophet to predict what I'm going to do next."

Chapter Sixteen

People meandered to the large, brick city hall on the corner as Evan stood across the street and rubbed a sweaty hand against his pant leg. Did he dare go in? If he was going to be an honest-to-goodness citizen of Sweetheart, he needed to stay informed about what was happening in town, and the monthly meeting was a great place to start.

He drew a bracing breath and crossed the road. An older couple approached the building at the same time. He held open a tall, bronze door for them. The woman squinted at him from behind wire-rimmed glasses, then her eyes widened in recognition. She'd been his Sunday school teacher back in the day.

"Mrs. Williams," he said. "Good to see you again."

She somehow nodded and tilted her nose in the air at the same time. Grasping her husband's arm tighter, Mrs. Williams entered without speaking. Evan followed the couple into what used to be the Sweetheart Memorial Bank. The historic architecture boasted marble tiles, a carved wooden staircase leading to a second floor with a balcony overlooking the lobby, and painted frescoes on the ceiling. Designed in the late 1800s, it exuded strength and stability. Katherine's idea to convert it into the city hall was pure genius. It gave Sweetheart an air of both respectability and historic significance.

He scanned the small crowd for Deanna, but she wasn't in sight. Metal folding chairs covered the ground floor. A short platform near the bottom of the stairs held a lectern and a large flat-screen television on a stand. Katherine stood near it, speaking with two older gentlemen.

A long table with a coffee urn and platters of cookies sat along the side of the room. Evan's stomach growled at the sight, reminding him he hadn't eaten since dessert with Deanna. There was time to grab a quick snack before the meeting began.

Once he made his way to the table, he placed two pieces of iced lemon cake on a small paper plate.

A clicking tongue sounded somewhere behind him. He turned, but the only people near him were two middle-aged women in matching floral dresses with their backs to him. The Dover sisters, if he remembered correctly. Funny. They looked exactly the same as they had in his boyhood, with a perpetual air of disapproval hovering over them. He pitied the poor stiff who'd earned their censure this time? Evan directed his attention to the refreshments and poured himself a cup of coffee.

"Imagine," a female voice in a snippy tone said. "You just can't satisfy *some* people. They live off the town for half their life and then help themselves again without so much as a by your leave."

Evan's spine tightened. He glanced over his shoulder, but the women weren't looking at him. Was he paranoid? They could be talking about anybody.

He carried his food to the last row of chairs and sat on the end, then balanced the cake plate on his knee. The coffee tasted good. Not too strong. Not too bitter. He finished it in three gulps and set the empty cup on the chair beside him. From the corner of his vision, he spotted a familiar floral print.

The tongue clicking started again. "*Some* people want to drain the town dry. You'd expect a person to have a natural amount of shame. I know if my father behaved that way, I wouldn't dare show my face in Sweetheart."

The words pinged against his skull like metal BBs. No doubt who they were referring to this time. His pulse, combined with a ringing, pounded in his ears. Nausea hit hard. Evan set his plate on the empty chair and rose on shaky legs.

This was what he'd expected from the beginning. But so many people had given him a free pass, he'd let his guard down. He'd been a fool to come. It was too soon to think he could be a part of Sweetheart. He hadn't paid his proper dues yet.

Although he kept his gaze lowered, he felt them. The eyes. Watching from every corner of the room. He knew they weren't all hostile. Some probably pitied him. He wasn't sure what was worse. The animosity could be attributed to his dad. But the pity? It seemed personal.

"Darling!"

A soft body tackled him from behind. The subtle scent of Deanna's perfume filled his nostrils, waking him from his stupor.

"I didn't see you come in since I was fixing refreshments in the kitchen." She spun him around with the finesse of a ballroom dancer and beamed up at him. "Can you give me a ride home later? My bicycle has a flat tire. Maybe I should let you give me those driving lessons you suggested."

"Lessons?" He peered at the room. As expected, everyone focused on them. "Right. How about tomorrow? We can practice in the supermarket parking lot or even the old pasture behind the ranch."

"Tomorrow?" She clasped her hands together. "I love a man who keeps his promises. You're one in a million, Evan Colter." Stretching on her tiptoes, she threw her arms around his neck and pressed her supple lips to his.

Evan forgot about the meeting. He forgot about the eyes. He forgot about the gossipy old women who were censuring them both. His brain threw away every coherent thought except one.

Deanna.

Her sweet mouth molded to his, reassuring, comforting, reminding him he wasn't alone in this battle.

His hands raised slowly. They settled at her waist, uncertain at first, not pushing her away but not pulling her closer either. They tested the moment, playing with the new emotion crackling inside of him like a Fourth of July sparkler.

Deanna.

She didn't feel like his little sister anymore. Or even the girl next door. She was a woman. A beautiful, vivacious, and captivating woman who had rushed to his side because someone was bullying him. Like the kid in third grade. Was that all he was to her? A charity case? Someone to be protected and pitied? His body stiffened. He might have pushed her away, but just then, her lips separated from his, and she whispered.

"Evan Colter, if you embarrass me in front of those spiteful old cats, I'll make you rue the day. You'd better kiss me like you mean it." Her clear gaze commanded, implored, and twinkled with humor at the same time.

He hesitated only an instant before crushing her to him and laying one on her as if they weren't in the middle of the town hall for half the population of Sweetheart to see. Cupping a palm at the back of her head, he angled his mouth over hers and thanked her with his lips for coming to his rescue. The folds of her poofy skirt enveloped his legs in a pillow-soft embrace. She felt warm and comforting and entirely different than the Dee he'd known his whole life.

A squealing microphone echoed in the large space, and Katherine Park spoke. "Can everyone please take a seat? The meeting is about to begin. And I do mean you, Deanna Day. You can kiss your boyfriend later. We have at least fifteen items on the agenda, and I don't want to be here until midnight. My feet are killing me."

Deanna pulled away by degrees, not a trace of embarrassment on her face. She smiled at him and winked. "Guess we'd better sit." She took his hand, led him to the seat he'd vacated, and picked up the dishes from the adjoining chair. Passing him the cake and cup, she sat beside him and whispered. "You're going to need this. These city council meetings drag on forever."

The meeting commenced. It lumbered through items about street signs and festivals and one particularly explosive point where two neighbors shouted at each other over whether or not roosters should be fostered within the city limits.

Evan stole glances at Deanna throughout the hour. She enjoyed the proceedings like a spectator at a football game. Her eyes crinkled at the corners when something struck her as funny. And an occasional pursing of her mouth drew his attention to the lips that had recently rocked his world.

Why, he couldn't say.

He'd kissed Deanna in the diner with no stronger emotions than gratitude and amusement. This second time ...

He cleared his throat and checked his paper coffee cup, but it was empty. Nothing to wash down the sudden discomfort.

Without looking at him, Deanna opened her box-shaped,

shiny red purse and passed him a cough drop. It was the sweet, cherry kind that probably contained zero medicinal benefits but sure tasted good.

Evan contemplated the lozenge before unwrapping the drop and popping it into his mouth. Life was sweeter with Deanna. But it was better not to get confused or allow himself to rely on her compassion and support. She might mistake it for romantic interest. And he could never allow himself to cause her pain.

Get your head on straight, Colter.

He couldn't use people the way his father had. Boundaries must be kept. That way, nobody got hurt.

Chapter Seventeen

Deanna poured a cup of sugar into a plastic pitcher of tea and stirred with quick, agitated strokes. Empty containers, cups, and dishes filled the large island in the middle of the city hall's kitchen. Elise Walker frittered behind her, refilling a platter with freshly baked chocolate chip cookies. Once the woman left the room, Deanna stopped mixing, covered her face, and groaned.

How could she force Evan to kiss her in front of the whole town? Not even giving him a choice in the matter. Katherine had been right. She was a shameless hussy.

Add that to their first kiss in the café and her serenade from the theater stage, and he might be sneaking out the door to Dallas. Or at the very least, calling the sheriff to report a stalker.

It's not like she was inexperienced in the area of romance. She'd dated plenty of men and mastered the art of refined flirting by the time she was eighteen. But her romantic overtures to Evan had been anything but subtle.

She should apologize. Deanna dropped the spoon and

whirled in frantic haste. Her elbow bumped the handle of the pitcher, and it tilted. She lunged. Too late.

Crash!

The plastic container hit the floor. Sweet tea gushed in every direction. A rich brown puddle spread.

"Oh no!" Deanna jumped as the cool liquid seeped through her shoes.

"Deanna Day." Mrs. Biddle's flaming burgundy head popped through the doorway. "What kind of mess have you made now?"

"Oh, you know." Deanna gave a bitter laugh. "The usual." She grabbed a dish towel and pushed it along the sea of sticky liquid leaking into the tile grooves. The puddle lapped around the tiny fabric and continued to spread. She raced to the cabinet, grabbed the entire roll of paper towels, and formed an absorbent barricade.

Evan appeared behind Mrs. Biddle. "What happened?"

"Deanna spilled a whole gallon of tea on the floor." Mrs. Biddle tsk-tsked. "That girl is the clumsiest thing I ever did see." Her voice faded as she walked away.

Deanna turned her back to Evan so he couldn't witness the forest fire blazing across her cheeks. She grabbed the hem of her poodle skirt and crouched, looking for a less-saturated spot to kneel and mop up everything.

"Stop!" Evan bolted to her side. "You'll ruin your clothes."

"It hardly matters. I've got to clean my mess."

"Just leave it to me." He gently tugged her away, crossed to the closet, and found a mop and bucket inside.

"I'll do it." Deanna shadowed his steps and reached for the mop.

He held it out of reach, extending his arm behind him. "Go out and mingle. I can manage this."

Evan picked up the empty container from the floor and set

it on the counter, then rolled up his sleeves and got to work. The veins in his muscular forearms bulged as he swabbed the floor, mopping at warp speed. The sizeable puddle of tea disappeared quickly.

On the sidelines, Deanna shifted from one foot to the other, unwilling to abandon him with a mess she'd created. If she couldn't help, at least she could stand there and suffer with him. Not that it was punishment to watch such a gorgeous man do a chore she hated. Cleaning had never been her forte. If she hadn't already been in love with him her whole life, she'd for sure be a goner after this.

"What's going on?" Elise poked her head through the doorway.

Deanna moaned. "I spilled tea all over the floor, and Evan volunteered to clean it up."

"What a sweet fiancé you've got there," she cooed. "I wish I could get my husband to clean."

Evan paused and leaned his arm on top of the mop. "You think I'm a keeper, Mrs. Walker?"

"No doubt about it." She poked a finger in Deanna's back. "You better reimburse him for that manual labor."

"Yes, ma'am." Deanna smiled. "I will."

"No time like the present."

Evan's face crinkled. "We're good, Mrs. Walker. Dee can *reimburse* me later."

"Don't rob an old woman of the chance to witness two young people in love." Elise sighed. "I lost track of the last time I enjoyed any romance of my own." She shoved Deanna toward Evan. "Go ahead, honey. Give him a little smooch."

Deanna stumbled. Her foot slid on the freshly mopped floor, and she catapulted forward. Evan dropped the mop and caught her against him. Her hand rested on his chest.

"Hope you don't mind," Deanna whispered. Two kisses in

one night. God must be on her side. She didn't give Evan the chance to respond before wrapping both arms around his neck, pulling him down, and kissing him as if it were her only chance. Truth be told, that fear was always at the back of her mind. Every time she got the opportunity to kiss Evan, her heart wondered if it would be the last.

But this kiss seemed different.

His lips were firm. But they somehow felt more, for lack of a better word, willing. Evan was kissing her like a man who actually found her attractive. Had she finally broken through the faux-sister barrier? She'd expected it to take longer.

"My, my, my," a female voice that wasn't Elise's intruded.

They broke contact and found Renae Smith lounging against one side of the entry. Elise had disappeared to who knew where. Deanna wished Renae would follow the older lady's example, but she just stood with one bright red fingernail tapping her chin.

Renae laughed. "I see you've figured out whether or not the beard scratches."

Deanna glared at her. "Do you need something?"

"Yep." She pushed away from the frame and approached them, then chose to stop closer to Evan than Deanna. "But not from you, from Evan. Didn't you say you were renovating your ranch to work with troubled youth?"

"That's right." He retrieved the mop and leaned it against the counter.

"Well, I've got one for you. How would you like to practice with my nephew, Marco?"

Deanna inched beside Evan and poked between his shoulder blades where Renae couldn't see. She'd heard about Marco Smith. Rumor had it, he was a handful and would probably be anything but cooperative.

Evan squirmed at her prodding finger. "I'm sorry. The ranch won't be ready for boarders until next year."

"Oh, I don't mean he has to live there." Renae swatted his arm. "But my sister is working two shifts lately, and Marco's using all that alone time to make some stupid choices. She's really worried about him, and we thought if he came and helped you, it might keep him out of trouble."

Deanna's eyes met Evan's. She didn't want him to be hassled. But this was what he planned to do with the ranch anyway. Either way, it was his decision.

He shrugged and faced Renae. "I suppose he could come by on Saturday. I was planning to power wash the outside of the barn and then paint it. He can help if he wants."

"Oh, he won't *want* to do anything. Trust me." Renae smirked. "But we won't give him a choice. I'll drop him by around ten in the morning."

"Fine." Evan nodded.

"Thanks, hot stuff. I'll grill you one of my famous T-bones sometime as a thank-you." Renae gave him a wink and left the kitchen.

Deanna's lower jaw jutted. She snatched the mop and carried it to the sink to rinse it out. "Are you sure you want to sign up for guard duty? From what I hear, Marco is a troublemaker."

"So was I at one time." Evan joined her, leaned back against the counter, and crossed his arms. "If someone hadn't given me a chance, I might have turned into worse. Maybe I can be that someone for Marco."

She shut off the tap and wrung the excess water from the mop. "How's a girl supposed to resist a soft-hearted, spill-cleaning hunk like you?" Her tone grew prickly. "Renae is more than ready to cook you dinner the moment you say the word, *hot stuff.*"

"I must admit, I love a good steak."

Deanna's eyes cut to him. "Feel free to try out her cooking whenever the mood hits you."

"Nah." He nudged her with his hip. "You keep me busy enough. I guess you'll have to grill that T-bone for me."

A tiny smile graced her lips. She dried her fingers on a nearby towel and bumped him back. "I'm a terrible cook. Everyone says so."

"Uh-oh." Evan laughed. "You've been hiding important information from me. What other secrets do you have?" He took the mop from the sink and carried it to the stoop to let it dry.

Had he missed the guilt that must be painting Deanna's face like cheap makeup? There was one secret she'd buried deep, and it was much worse than being a terrible cook. This one, he wouldn't be able to laugh off.

By the time Evan returned, she'd schooled her features into pleasant nonchalance. Someday she'd tell him. But not yet. He was starting to accept her as a woman instead of a sister. Deanna knew it was wrong, but she couldn't ruin this wonderful development with something so inconvenient as the truth.

Chapter Eighteen

Twenty years of memories and sentimental junk took a long time to pack.

Friday morning was almost gone when Evan loaded the last of Mrs. Hammington's things into the moving truck and closed the heavy metal door. He walked around the side and waited as Deanna escorted the little old lady across the front yard. Deanna wore a pink plaid shirt tucked into old-fashioned bell-bottom jeans. A matching bandanna covered her hair. The ladies joined him, and Mrs. H turned to the house for another look.

"Me and my husband loved it here." She patted Evan's sleeve. "We took good care of the place. Now it's up to you and Deanna to carry on the tradition."

His conscience pinged as it always did when someone mentioned their phony engagement. "Mrs. H, we're not—"

"Let's get a move on." She opened the passenger side, hauled herself onto the seat, and slammed the door, cutting off any attempt at explanation.

Deanna shook her head. "Better not keep her waiting. Mr. Walker and his nephews are supposed to meet you at her sister's place to help unload. I think Mrs. H will be much happier in town."

"Are you sure you don't want to go with us?"

"I've got plenty to keep me occupied until you get back. I'm dying to check out the hayloft in the barn. Mrs. H told me there are all sorts of antique goodies stored there. Maybe I'll even find some of your old family heirlooms."

"Be careful on the ladder. Who knows how rickety it is." Evan walked around the front of the truck. "I'll be back in a few hours."

A few hours extended to five as Evan helped unload Mrs. Hammington's furniture at her sister's place and then rearranged it multiple times for the indecisive women. Afterward, he picked up hamburgers at The Brunch Café for Deanna and himself, hoping she wasn't too upset at how long he'd deserted her.

He drove past the Dover sisters on Main Street. The older women jerked their faces away when they recognized him. They wore the same sour expressions as they had at the civic meeting. Even then, they'd made it plain that they didn't approve of his return, but the snub still burned.

For a century, since his great-great-granddaddy Amos P. Colter built the town single-handedly, the name of Colter had been a symbol of honor. How long would it take for him to redeem the family in the regard of Sweetheart's citizens? Was it even possible? Or was he a fool for trying?

Perhaps the town had changed too much. Perhaps *he* had changed too much.

Evan drove for a while until he reached the turnoff for the ranch. After bumping along the dirt road to the house, he parked the truck and exited with the food bag. As he slammed the door, a high-pitched shriek echoed from the barn. He dropped the burgers and bolted toward the sound. Was Deanna hurt?

Before he reached the barn, she zipped from the wide-open doors and rushed past him, ripping the bandanna from her golden curls and shaking her head upside down.

"Spiders!" she squealed. "A whole family landed on me."

Her body gyrated in a frantic shimmy. Her comical dance swept the cobwebs of the past from his thoughts. She was so ridiculous. But she'd always been ridiculous, ever since they were children. He liked that about her. It reminded him there was one thing unchanged about Sweetheart. The undiluted sunshine that was Deanna Day remained the same.

She bent her arms behind her and slapped her spine. "Do you see them? Are they skittering all over me?" She jiggled and ducked around the yard.

He'd escaped a lecture for his long absence thanks to the creepy-crawlies.

Evan's lips twitched. "Mmmm. Yeah. There's dozens."

"What?" Deanna's brows rose almost to her hairline. She spun in a frenzied circle, clawing at her back. "Where? Get them off!"

"Too many. I guess you're a goner."

She halted and glared at him. "Evan Colter, I can knock you off your feet if I want to. I know judo."

"So you've informed me. But I wouldn't be surprised if spiders aren't the worst critters hiding in the barn. You should stop treasure hunting."

Her smile reappeared. "That reminds me. I found the most amazing thing. Come and see." She grabbed his hand and towed him into the ancient building, past dusty machinery and piles of boxes, to a spot in the corner. With both arms, she gestured. "Ta-da!"

He squinted at the half-unrolled heavy fabric in front of

him. The embroidery showed a dance scene with people dressed in tunics and long dresses, cavorting around a field. "I don't understand. Why are you excited about a carpet?"

"Don't you get it? This is perfect for our Sweet Shakes Weekend."

"The Shakespeare festival? Why?"

"This year's theme is highlights from his works. We're mostly playing it for comedy, but the finale is straight tragedy. I'm doing the death scene from *Romeo and Juliet* again. For a year, I've been dreaming of redemption and the chance to say my lines without sopping wet hair hanging in my eyes. Imagine this gorgeous tapestry stretched across the back of the stage while I die for love." Deanna mimicked stabbing the blade in her chest. "'O happy dagger!'"

Evan turned away and rummaged in a crate of odds and ends while she continued.

"'This is thy sheath; there rust, and let me die.'" Deanna clapped with glee. "The tapestry will be the perfect backdrop as I take one last kiss from Romeo's still-warm lips."

"Kiss?" Evan pulled out a beat-up metal canteen. "Didn't you say Boone Richardson was playing Romeo?"

"He already has the costume since he was Romeo last year. It took me forever to convince him to wear the tights."

"Didn't you dump him?"

"As a date, yes. As a scene partner, no. We've been rehearsing for a month. Why?" She waggled her brows. "Does it bug you?"

"Makes no difference to me one way or the other." He chucked the canteen in the box. "I just hope it doesn't give Boone false hope after you went to the trouble of breaking it off."

"How so?"

Evan sat on the edge of the crate and stretched his legs in

front of him. "Men are simple creatures, Dee. Physical contact stirs us up. It may be acting for you, but Boone might let some real feelings get mixed in during your kiss scene."

"It won't be a real kiss, silly. We were always going to fake it."

"Fake it? How?"

Deanna laughed. "Actors use all sorts of tricks on the stage. For example,"—she flittered over and pressed a small hand against his bearded cheek—"you gaze deeply into each other's eyes, like this."

Her face drew close to his. Evan's pulse kicked into higher gear. Odd. It used to be, he'd felt nothing stronger than surprise when Deanna kissed him. But that hadn't been the case on the last occasion. Her mouth came near enough, her soft breath brushed his skin.

"Then right before the actual smooch—" Deanna moved her thumb 'til it was blocking his lips and laid her mouth on top of it. "Mwah. No contact necessary." She giggled as she stepped away. "It's especially handy when you're acting with someone who hasn't brushed their teeth."

His heartbeat returned to its normal tempo, but it still annoyed him that the brief contact affected him at all. Evan stood and patted the dust from his jeans. "Why bother? From what I hear, you've dated quite a few men in town."

Deanna stilled. "Excuse me?"

"If you've already kissed them offstage, might as well make it real when there's an audience."

No immediate response followed. He looked up to find a flushed Deanna. Her hands clenched at her sides.

"Evan Colter, I could flatten you for those words. How dare you."

"What?" He rubbed the back of his neck. "I was kidding."

She advanced until they stood toe to toe. "For your

information, the only man in this town—in fact, the only man on this planet—who's ever had the privilege of tasting my lips is you." She poked his chest. "You big lunkhead."

"But what about the truckload of men you dated?"

"I dated them. I didn't kiss them. Now I'm kind of wishing I had. It certainly wasn't because I was too shy. I just never hankered to kiss anyone but you, for all the good it's done me. Oh, I'm so mad, I ought to pin your ears back." She spun on her heel and stalked away, shouting, "Bring that tapestry to the house. I'm going to take it to town with me. I figure it's the least you can do after leaving me here alone to do all your dirty work." Without another glance his way, she stomped from the barn.

Looked like he hadn't escaped without retribution after all. Evan's lips twitched as he watched her go. She sure was cute when she was mad. No wonder a gang of fellows had camped outside her door. With a cheerful whistle, he propped the dusty carpet on his shoulder and hurried after her.

"Hey, Spitfire. Wait up."

Chapter Nineteen

The ranch house kitchen window framed a majestic array of sunset colors, painting the clouds in the wide, uninterrupted sky. It stretched for miles without an airplane or skyscraper to mar the beauty. Evan's soul breathed a sigh of relief. He'd always hated living in the big city.

Every muscle in his body ached. After nine hours of moving Mrs. Hammington's furniture and then cleaning out the barn for what remained of the afternoon, he was ready for a break. Deanna, on the other hand, had insisted on riding her bike home instead of letting him drive her. Where did she get the energy?

He perused the plastic containers of food she'd left for him, chose a dish of macaroni and cheese mixed with ham, and warmed it in the microwave. When it was ready, he unwrapped a plastic fork left over from some takeout and poured himself a tall glass of sweet tea from the gallon Deanna made at lunchtime. After walking outside to the front porch, Evan settled on the top step with his legs stretched in front of him. He took a bite of food, chewed, and paused. It was ... crunchy. How did someone mess up mac 'n' cheese? Laughing to himself, he set the dish aside and grabbed his drink. Taking a swig, he savored the cool, tasty liquid. Not too syrupy with a brisk little kick at the end. Just the way he liked it. Deanna might be a terrible cook, but she made good tea. Evan downed the rest of the drink in four gulps.

The old Double Heart Ranch belonged to him. He was finally home. The deed was in the dresser drawer, and his clothes hung in the closet. But something was missing. It nagged at his insides like a mosquito. The sense that he'd left an important detail undone.

But what?

A cloud of dust kicked up in the distance, and a large white SUV appeared. He didn't recognize the car. It couldn't be Deanna since she didn't drive, Renae wasn't supposed to bring her nephew by until tomorrow morning, and Evan hadn't invited anyone else to the ranch.

The vehicle stopped near the house. Its door opened, and a short woman in a stonewashed denim pantsuit with hot pink cowboy boots and matching sunglasses emerged. Lanette Johnson. Why was she here?

"Hey, sugar!" she called.

Evan thunked his empty glass on the porch and drew his legs onto the lower step. What made the clueless woman think she was welcome? Had she forgotten what part she played in wrecking his family? He sat on the front stoop, eyes pointed at the dusty ground.

Lanette approached and settled beside him, leaving a foot of space between them. "I saw Cora Biddle in town. She told me you've moved in now."

He remained silent.

"It's good to see you, Evan," she said in a softer voice.

If he refused to answer, would she take the hint and leave? She didn't.

"Word around town is, you and Deanna were smooching in the city hall kitchen. People are laying bets on when the wedding will be. Is it true?"

Obviously, the silent treatment wasn't working. But he had no desire to explain to Lanette his complicated relationship with his fake fiancée.

"And if it is?" he asked.

"If it is, I'll throw you both the biggest engagement party you've ever seen. You two are like my own kids. It hurts me how much of your life I've missed." She reached a bejeweled hand toward him but paused at the last moment. "When I heard you were back in Sweetheart, I was hoping you'd come to the house. Harry and I were waiting for you to make the first move—not sure if you wanted to talk to us."

He snorted. "Can you understand why?"

"Naturally." She crossed her short legs at the ankles. The rhinestones on her pink cowboy boots flashed in the fading sunlight. "We were the ones who exposed your Daddy's crimes."

"Yeah, thanks for that."

"It took us forever to make the decision. We'd been friends with y'all for so long—the best of friends. Like family. It seemed inconceivable that we could do anything to hurt you all. But your daddy chose a dark path, and someone had to stop him."

Evan's jaw clenched. "I know he deserved what he got. My dad did terrible things. But I can't help wishing ..." He raked his fingers through his hair. "Wasn't there some other way than having him arrested? Couldn't you have confronted him?"

"We tried." She picked at a loose fiber on her pants. "More

than once. But he refused to accept what he was doing was wrong."

"Still,"—Evan faced her—"how could you do that to me and mom? I thought you and Uncle Harry loved us."

"We did." Lanette turned her body his way and patted his knee. "We *do*. But we also loved Sweetheart. And if we had let your Daddy keep leading it down the wrong detour, there would have been nothing left. You remember what a mess it was then. Drugs. Violence. People afraid to leave their houses after dark."

Evan concentrated on the road, his threaded fingers hanging between his knees. "I don't remember any of that."

"You were too young. You only saw the good parts of Sweetheart. But take my word for it, things were falling apart. Harry and I couldn't let that happen, for all our sakes."

"One day, I had a loving family, lots of friends, and a beautiful home. The next, my mom was pitching our suitcases in the trunk of the car and driving us as far from Sweetheart and my father as she could get."

Lanette nodded. "It must have been torture for Marion. She always hated confrontation."

Memories, both the good and the bad, hung like an invisible curtain between them. There was no way to forget the happy times he'd spent with the woman beside him. She'd been a second mother to him. That was what made her betrayal unbearable.

Evan shoved off the step and stood. He glared at her with a barely controlled rage shaking his insides. "I know you did the right thing. And I know I'm being unreasonable to resent you for it. But I can't help it. My world collapsed in an instant because of you."

She joined him and reached out, but he jerked away.

Her hand lowered. "I'm sorry. All these years, I've

wondered how you were. How your momma was. Prayed you'd both found happiness somewhere else."

"Happiness?" He scoffed. "Oh, Mom's plenty happy. She found a new husband, a new social circle, and picked up right where she left off with fancy luncheons and charity bazaars, as if nothing ever happened." He pounded a fist against his chest. "I was the one who paid the price. Living like a refugee. Never fitting in anywhere."

Tears pooled in Lanette's eyes. They spilled over the heavily mascaraed edges and streaked runny black trails down her cheeks. "What else can I say, Evan?" She clutched his arm. "I don't blame you for hating me. But that won't stop me from caring about you, from checking on you, from trying to be a part of your life. No matter how long it takes for you to forgive me."

His spine stiffened. "You might get awfully tired of waiting."

She released him. "I'm sorry for the years you suffered. I wish I'd have known where you were so I could help. But you're back now, and that's what matters most. Sweetheart is where you belong. You take as much time as you need. I'll still be here when you're ready." She headed to her car, then opened the door and hollered, "By the way, I hope you make those engagement rumors true. I pray this is the start of a whole new life for you and Deanna."

Lanette climbed into her vehicle and drove away. Evan lingered in front of the steps, staring at the twilight sky. The last remains of the sun were disappearing on the horizon, and the shadows stretched into the darkening clouds.

A new life?

He wanted one more than anything. Returning to Sweetheart was supposed to accomplish the miracle. He had defied his fears and ignored the naysayers, bought the family ranch, and even found himself a fiancée—temporary though she might be. But none of those things gave him the feeling he craved.

His glorious homecoming was missing the *home* part. No matter how hard he tried, Evan still felt like a stranger. And he didn't know how to fix that.

Chapter Twenty

Deanna collapsed on Katherine's charcoal-gray sofa, leaned her head against the back cushion, and moaned. "I'm more worn out than a chaperone at a sock hop."

Katherine settled beside her and pulled a pillow onto her lap. "No wonder. If I had chased my husband as hard as you're chasing Evan, I'd be exhausted too."

"Who are you kidding?" Deanna made duck lips at her. "I was there for your courtship. You went after Ryan with all the subtlety of a steamroller."

"True. But look where it got me." She stretched her arms wide. "Living in my dream cottage with the man I love and our precious son."

A fussy wail sounded from the bedroom, and Deanna smirked. "There's Mr. Precious now."

"Sounds like Aaron refuses to take his nap." Katherine hurried down the hall and reappeared a moment later, bouncing the one-year-old on her hip.

"Dee-dee-dee-dee!" He launched forward, arms stretched wide to Deanna.

"Yes, Aunt Dee's here." Katherine set him on the floor. "Go play with her awhile."

Deanna knelt on the carpet as Aaron toddled her way with an enormous smile. She scooped him up and covered his face with kisses. He squealed, his chunky body wriggling against her torso.

Katherine relaxed on the couch and laid a hand on her belly. "Anybody who says it's easier having your kids close together is a liar." She flopped to the side, her head landing on the armrest.

"So why did you?"

"You think I planned either pregnancy?" she scoffed. "Aaron was an accident. But this second time was an act of God. Even birth control failed me. I didn't realize antibiotics decreased their effectiveness. My babies were determined to come into the world."

"Wait a minute." Deanna sat next to Katherine. "Babies? As in plural?"

"Yes." Katherine moaned. "We found out yesterday. I will soon give birth to twin boys."

"Wow." Deanna locked both arms around Aaron's tummy as he fidgeted on her lap. "Do you suppose they'll have as much energy as their big brother?"

"Let's hope at least one takes after their laid-back father."

Deanna laughed, and Aaron joined her. His high-pitched giggle did funny things to her insides. What would it be like to hold a squirming tornado of energy that belonged to her?

Evan and her.

As if Katherine read her mind, she asked, "How's it going with your long-lost love?"

Deanna sighed. "He's still relegating me to the little sister category."

"Not good."

"No, it's not. But I can't solve the mystery of how to break out of it. I've tried wearing my prettiest outfits, flirting so outrageously that even *I'm* embarrassed, cooking his favorite dishes—"

"Wait a minute." Katherine sat straight. "You cooked for him? Are you trying to make him leave town?"

"Remind me to throw a pillow at your head once you aren't pregnant."

Aaron slithered off Deanna's lap to the floor and crawled over where Katherine's Yorkshire terriers lay on their bed. The female, Bella, saw him coming and raced for the kitchen, but the more chill Romeo remained and allowed the baby to pat him with a clumsy hand.

Katherine rubbed her back. "Have you tried laying another one on him? That's how I got Ryan's attention."

"We've kissed three times since Evan got home. Nothing too spicy, but still—"

"Hold up." Katherine bounced in place. "Three whole times? Congratulations! What did Evan say about the lip-locks?"

"Nothing." Deanna crossed her arms. "He never even brought them up."

"I don't know, my friend. It doesn't sound too—No, Aaron! Put the dog down."

Katherine careened off the couch and caught Romeo as he slipped from the baby's grasp. Aaron waddled to Deanna and raised his arms. She caught him up and placed another kiss on his chubby cheek. He laid his head on her shoulder and yawned.

"Someone's sleepy," she said.

"Finally," his mother said. "His naptime was supposed to be an hour ago." She returned to the couch.

Deanna rocked the toddler back and forth. "I long to have

what you do—a home of my own, babies, a husband. But only with Evan. It's always been him and only him."

"Why? You've dated a truckload of guys in the years he's been gone. Why haven't any of those men made you forget him?"

"God alone can answer that." Deanna shrugged. "It's like my heart has one key, and I gave it to Evan a long time ago."

"Did you steal that cheesy line from one of those black-and-white movies you watch?"

"Nope." Deanna laughed. "It's one hundred percent me. I'm an old-fashioned girl, through and through."

"Then don't give up." Katherine slapped her knees. "Find out what makes Evan see you as a woman instead of a little sister and crank it up to the max."

The baby's breathing slowed against Deanna's chest, and she ducked her head to take a peek. "I think he fell asleep."

Katherine's whisper was barely audible. "Thank the Lord. Don't you dare move for the next two hours."

Deanna settled against the couch, and they sat in the peaceful living room without speaking—the comfortable silence of old friends. But the thoughts began to swirl in her brain. Evan's reappearance had recalled not only the old memories but the guilt of the past. It weighed heavily on her, demanding release.

"There's one more thing standing in the way." She spoke quietly so as not to wake Aaron. "Even if Evan fell for me, I'm terrified he wouldn't be able to accept it."

Katherine turned her head Deanna's way. "What?"

"Something I've done. Or did. A long time ago. When we were kids."

"I've known you since diaper days. I seriously doubt there's anything you could have done that was unforgivable."

"I've never told you this." Deanna picked at the gray piping on the couch cushion. "It was when we were young. Right before the scandal broke about Evan's dad."

"That was a wretched period."

"Yes, and—" Deanna gulped. "It was all my fault."

"What do you mean?" Katherine gave Deanna her full attention. "How could what his father did possibly be your fault?"

"Not that. But … but the fact everyone found out was because of me. I was at Evan's house one night. We were playing hide-and-seek."

"Hold up. Hide-and-seek? Weren't you a teenager then?"

"Thirteen." Deanna shrugged. "What can I say? I liked the idea of Evan chasing me. The game was my idea, of course, and I'd stowed away inside that huge armoire in his father's study. It was taking Evan forever to find me. I must have been in there for fifteen minutes." She held Aaron tighter. "Then Mayor Colter came in, and I heard him on the phone. He was talking about drugs and setting up a meeting with someone at the old Hatcher farm at midnight."

Katherine leaned closer, her voice hushed. "Did he find out you were listening?"

"No. Mayor Colter left the room without finding me. I wasn't sure exactly what the conversation meant, but I knew it was something bad. I hid in the armoire for a while. Honestly, I was scared, almost to the point of hyperventilating. When I left the house, Uncle Harry and Aunt Lanette were standing in the front yard. I started crying and told them everything. They said they'd take care of it, and then Aunt Lanette drove me home. The next day, it was all over town, the police caught Mayor Colter with drug dealers." Deanna rubbed her face. "It got crazy from there. The rumors. The scandal. The trial."

Katherine nodded. "I remember. But do you really believe that was because of you? The mayor had been involved in shady stuff for years. People already suspected him."

"Maybe so, but I don't think it's a coincidence he was arrested the day after I told on him. Do you?"

Katherine didn't answer the question. Instead, she reached for Deanna's hand. "Regardless of how he was exposed, it was his criminal activities that caused his downfall. Not you."

Deanna gnawed on her lip. "But that night destroyed Evan's life. *I* destroyed Evan's life. How can he ever forgive me for the part I played?"

Yip. Yip. Yip.

Bella ran from the kitchen. She plowed into the dog bed and woke the sleeping Romeo, who barked in annoyance at his sister. Aaron jolted in Deanna's arms and whimpered.

"Oh boy," his mother said. "Here we go."

The pudgy baby's cheeks screwed up, and he let loose an unearthly yowl. Deanna turned Aaron so he was facing her. He clung to her neck and sobbed.

The front door opened, and Ryan walked into the living room. "What's all the commotion?"

"Thank goodness you're home." Katherine rose to meet him. "Your son is having a meltdown. Again."

"My son?" Ryan crossed the room and kissed her. "His passionate temper tantrums remind me an awful lot of someone else I know."

She slapped his chest but didn't deny it.

Bella raced to Katherine's side and pawed at her leg. Katherine retrieved the tiny Yorkie and glared at her. "This is your fault, you scamp. It was peaceful until you woke Aaron up. No puppy treats tonight."

Deanna rocked on the couch. The weight of her confession dissolved among the chaos of the crying baby, barking dogs, and grumpy pregnant friend's complaints. She patted Aaron on the back and cooed.

Would she ever have a home full of noisy love like this one? Or would she be doomed to old maidenhood because the one man she wanted was the one man she'd betrayed?

Chapter Twenty-One

Saturday morning dawned early for Evan. The sun was barely visible when he fired up the power washer and got to work on the south side of the barn. By the time Deanna pedaled her bike past the gate at ten o'clock, he'd completed the section they would be painting. She was dressed in her version of work clothes, some sort of vintage, wide-legged overalls with a red-and-white checkered shirt and a matching bandanna over her hair.

After he put the washer away, they waited on the front porch for the arrival of their new helper. The temperature had lowered during the night, and the regular humidity was replaced by a refreshing breeze.

Deanna leaned over the railing and peered at the fluffy clouds drifting in the sky. "What a perfect day for painting."

Evan checked the time on his phone before slipping it into his pocket. "Renae's running late. I got the power washing out of the way, and I hope we can get one side of the barn done today."

"What color did you choose?"

"Forest green."

"Not red? You rebel."

Tires squealed in the distance. Dust flew from churning wheels as a scarlet coupe turned onto the long drive. It barreled down the road and screeched to a halt in front of the house.

Renae emerged. She walked around to the passenger side, opened the door, and hollered. "Get out of the car! I've gotta get to work."

The teen inside didn't move.

She thumped the roof. "You don't want to spend all day at the salon watching old ladies get their hair done, do you?"

A young man around fourteen climbed slowly from the vehicle. He wore a wrinkled T-shirt, ragged jeans, and a ball cap pulled low over curly black hair. His dark eyes glared from under the hat's brim.

Renae towed him across the yard to where Evan and Deanna stood. "This is Marco. He doesn't have much experience with manual labor, or any labor for that fact, but feel free to put him to work." She frowned at her nephew. "Aren't you gonna hug me goodbye?"

Marco looked at her like she had three heads.

"Don't act so cold to your favorite aunt." She grabbed him in a strong embrace and squeezed tightly as he squirmed. "Be good now." She released him and waved at the other adults. "This is Evan and Deanna. If you make any trouble for them, I'll be sure you regret it."

The boy made a sarcastic sound.

She smirked. "You might not have noticed, but I just picked your pocket." Renae flourished a silver phone.

He scowled and swiped for the cell.

His taller aunt held it high above her head. "If you ever want to see your phone again, you'll do what they tell you."

She gave one last nod to Deanna and Evan, then hurried to her car, jumped inside, and drove away.

"Hello, Marco." Evan extended a hand for him to shake. "Ready to get to work?"

The teen chewed, open-mouthed, on a giant wad of lime-green gum. His apathetic gaze wandered, focusing on anything but the adults. He exhaled a long, bored breath.

Deanna and Marco were almost the same height. She blinked at the surly boy, crossed one arm in front of her, and rested the hand on her hip. Discomfort showed in her expression.

Evan tamped down a laugh at his new "helper." It was like staring in a mirror from eighteen years ago. The defiant posture and the bitterness in Marco's eyes reminded Evan of himself when he'd arrived at the boys' ranch.

"Fine." Evan withdrew his hand. "If you don't want to talk, you don't have to. How about you relax? Dee and I will have all the fun ourselves. You may be hanging around for a while." He took Deanna by the elbow and led her away.

"Is it okay to leave him there?" she whispered.

"Where's he going to go? The house is locked, and I doubt he'll feel the urge to wander in the woods."

They both checked on their protégé. Marco slumped to a sitting position on the steps. He spat his gum on the ground, yanked the bill of his ball cap even lower, and leaned his head against the porch railing.

Deanna bit her lower lip. "Aren't you going to make him help?"

Evan kept walking and shook his head. "If I do that, work becomes a punishment. I'd rather he see it as a reward. They did the same to me the first day I came to the ranch. I stomped around, angry at everything and everybody, declaring they couldn't make me do nothin'. Pop Wilson was the boss. He made it clear my attitude wouldn't fly and said if I wanted to get in on the interesting stuff, I'd have to sweeten my tone. I lasted about two days before I was bored out of my mind. Feeding cows and fixing fences started to look pretty good when there wasn't anything else to do."

They arrived at the barn, and Deanna picked up a paintbrush. "This Pop Wilson sounds like a wise man."

"The best. He saved my life." Evan bent and opened the lid of a paint can. "If I can do that for even one young man who's headed down the wrong path, all of Pop's effort wasn't in vain."

DEANNA TRIED TO PICTURE EVAN AS A SULLEN, REBELLIOUS TEENAGER, but it didn't compute. As a boy, he'd been a ray of sunshine, friendly to everyone, with a faith in God that ran bone deep. It was true that the grown-up version of him was quieter and less spiritual, but he still projected an air of dependability and honor. What other kind of man would devote his home to helping troubled teens like Marco?

The boy on the porch stretched out on the top step and tucked one arm under his head to take a nap. He tapped his sneaker against the post. His lazy posture telegraphed his intention to do anything but help.

She stuck her brush in the forest-green paint and spread a streak on the side of the barn. The wood was in fairly good condition, and the color went on easily. Marco was far enough away that he couldn't hear their conversation, and she was dying to know more about Evan's plans for the ranch. "What kind of activities are you planning for the boys?"

"After I get everything fixed up, we'll have animals they'll care for. I'll teach them how to ride a horse. There will be a garden for them to work in and regular duties like cooking and cleaning. It will be a community."

"Or a family." Deanna smiled.

"Exactly." He stopped painting. "Some of the harder cases will have little to no experience with a loving home. I hope they'll find that here."

Deanna laid her brush on top of the bucket and pressed her fingers to her eyes. Tears burned the back of her lids. This wasn't the time to be getting emotional. They had work to do.

"What's wrong?" Evan asked.

"Nothing," she eked out. "It's such an inspiring vision, it makes me get all choked up." She swiped the tears away. "I hope you'll let me help."

"What do you want to be in charge of? Riding? Carpentry? Cooking?"

"Definitely not cooking." She laughed. "We don't want the boys to run away. How about a dance class?"

"Dancing?" Evan thumbed at the teen lounging on the porch. "Guys like Marco won't go for that."

"They will if you tell them it impresses girls. And it will also help teach them social skills."

He laid his paintbrush beside hers. "It's not a bad idea. They could learn how to act like gentlemen."

"I'd give them tips on how to treat a lady, how to ask her to dance, how to dress up for a date."

"How to write a sappy love letter."

"You're never going to let me live that one down. Are you?"

"Why should I?" He grinned.

"What a relief you didn't keep it. I can imagine what kind of embarrassing, melodramatic phrases my emotional sixteen-year-old self used."

He half turned his body away and rubbed his nose. "I guess

that's a no to the letter-writing course, but let's keep the dancing."

She clapped. "This could be so much fun."

"Only someone like you would think of smoothing the sharp edges off delinquent teens as fun."

"What can I say? I'm an optimist. And this worthy mission of yours makes me want to be a part. I wish the naysayers in town truly understood what you were planning. Then they'd be as excited as I am."

Evan cast her a doubtful look. "I wish that were true."

"It is. Just give them a chance. Sweetheart folks are a bunch of softies. Even the critics will come around when they see how beautiful your dream for this place is."

Deanna soaked in the majesty of the Double Heart Ranch. Acres of pastureland rested behind the house, and a stretch of towering trees lined the perimeter. The newly applied streaks of forest-green paint glistened in the morning sunlight and blended into the natural setting.

Evan placed his hands on his hips. "What about *your* dream?"

"What do you mean?"

"Have you given any more thought to renovating the old theater?"

She twisted the toe of her shoe in the dirt. "Thought, yes. I even pitched the idea to Katherine, and our dear mayor was receptive. But when it comes to action, I can't seem to work up the nerve."

He laughed out loud.

"What?"

"If there's one thing you possess in spades, it's nerve."

She fussed with her bandanna, tugging it tighter over her hair. "Maybe I've been faking it all these years."

"Not a chance." Evan took her by the elbows. "If this is your dream, Dee, I'll support you like you've done for me. Don't doubt yourself. What you have to do is tap into that inner spitfire who's always threatening to knock me off my feet."

His warm acceptance threatened to melt her on the spot.

She gave him a wavery smile. "Thanks."

"Don't mention it." He released her. "Now, let's get back to work."

Deanna bent to retrieve her brush but popped up again. "Oooh! I had another brainstorm. Why don't you start a judo class with the boys?"

Evan cringed. "That's not such a good idea. Some of them probably ended up in the system because of fighting."

"Judo isn't about fighting. It's about learning self-discipline so a fight is unnecessary. Physical strength should be saved as a last resort."

"Still. Who could we get to teach the course?"

"Um, hello?" Deanna opened her arms wide. "I earned my black belt three years ago. How many times have I told you I could knock you off your feet if I wanted to?"

He chuckled. "Forgive me for doubting, but most of the boys will come from a rough lifestyle. They know how to defend themselves. I doubt they'd need you to teach them anything." Evan patted her head.

Deanna's eyes narrowed to slits. She grabbed his arm, spun so her back faced him, locked her shoulder under his armpit, and dropped to her knees. His weight followed her momentum, and she flipped him in an instant. He landed with a hard thud on the grass. She stretched one arm across his chest to rest her palm on the ground and leaned close. Her escaped curls tickled his jaw.

She peeked at the porch where a sleeping Marco lay oblivious to their unusual position, then returned her attention to Evan. "Good thing your protégé decided to take a nap, or we wouldn't be having nearly as much fun. Don't you agree martial arts can be an invigorating thing?"

He swallowed. "When did you learn judo again?"

"A few years ago. Right after I finished ballroom dancing lessons. If you think I'm good at one-arm shoulder throws, wait 'til you see me do the foxtrot." With a wink, she leaned away from him, stood, and helped him to his feet. "What do you say? Can I teach the boys dancing *and* judo?"

"Dancing? Yes." He brushed the dirt from his jeans. "Judo? Absolutely not."

Deanna crossed her arms. "Have I not proven myself capable? Should I offer another demonstration?"

"No, thank you." Evan held up both hands in surrender. "My vertebrae can't take it. I admit, you're more than capable, but there's another problem."

She leveled a suspicious glare his way. "What?"

"Deanna, if you get that close to the boys, I'm afraid they'll all fall in love with you. I can't have you breaking every heart on the ranch."

Her jaw slackened.

He chucked her under the chin and headed for the house.

Breaking hearts?

Was Evan Colter flirting with her? Deanna pressed her paint-splotched fingers to her lips and uttered a tiny squeal. Exhilaration coursed through her limbic system. A lifelong dream was coming true right in front of her eyes. The sweet taste of success made her hungry for more, and an unexpected picture of the old theater flashed in her mind. Were there other dreams she might try making a reality?

Did she have the courage?

Chapter Twenty-Two

Deanna sat at the kitchen table with her mother. She twirled her fork in the pasta, unable to swallow a bite of the spaghetti aglio e olio. The savory mix of olive oil and parmesan cheese was usually her favorite, but the prospect of hurting her sweet momma killed her appetite.

Ever since she'd stood on the old theater's stage and sung to Evan, the idea of buying the building and renovating it had hovered in her thoughts like a hazy fog. Over the weekend, he'd prodded her to make that hidden desire a reality in the same way he was doing with the ranch. His sweet affirmations were touching and a tad annoying at the same time. They forced her to consider what was holding her back.

It was the same issue she'd claimed her mom struggled with.

Change.

The word terrified and exhilarated her. What if her mother couldn't find someone to run the soda fountain museum in Deanna's stead? Or worse, what if the very suggestion disappointed her?

"You're awfully quiet," her mom said in a soft voice. "Thinking about Evan again?"

Deanna laughed. "That would be a natural assumption. Believe it or not, it's something different this time."

"Having a tough day at work?"

"Hardly." Deanna knew this was the opening she needed, but how to begin? She cleared her throat. "There wasn't much business. That's why I came home for lunch. It's been slow of late, and I wondered—I mean, I was thinking perhaps …" She set her fork down and twisted her fingers on her lap. "How would you feel about getting someone else to run the museum?"

Her mom blinked. "Where are you going to work instead?"

"I know this is out of the blue, but"—Deanna gulped—"I was considering taking out a loan to buy the old theater on Main Street. It still has life left in it. If I revamped the place, we could use it for the community productions."

"The theater?" Her mom's brow wrinkled. "Could you make a living with that?"

"The basement underneath is loaded with character. All the beautiful red brick walls and exposed pipes would make a fabulous banquet hall. I could rent it out for weddings and things. I bet lots of people are dying to hold their special events at such a historic, picturesque place. I could even advertise it in the bigger cities as a destination wedding option. The way people go crazy for good photo ops these days, I could make a ton of money, and …" It struck Deanna that her mother hadn't said a word, staring at her with wide eyes. "Do I sound crazy?"

"How are you going to pay for this?"

Not a word about her banquet hall plans. Deanna's confidence plunged. Every question her mother asked was practical and pointed. She must be worrying that her daughter was a sentimental fool.

Deanna slumped in her chair. "You're right. It would take a fortune."

"That's not what I said." Her mom reached across the table and tapped a finger on the wood. "I asked how you would pay for it."

"I have a good amount in my account. Remember, Grandma left me $20,000 when she passed away? And I've added to it over the years. Living at home. Not having to maintain a car or pay for gas. There weren't too many expenses, and I built my savings to around $47,000. That's not enough to purchase the building outright, but I hoped it would impress Mr. Amador at the bank. If I sell him on the idea of restoring the theater and bringing more business to Sweetheart, he might consider giving me a loan."

Her mom took a long, slow drink of coffee. She studied Deanna as she set the mug down, rose from her chair, and went into the other room. She reappeared with her purse on her arm.

"We'd better get going. Tony Amador has a tendency to clock out early. We want to catch him before he starts packing up."

"What?" Deanna stood. "You mean you're not mad I'm leaving the museum?"

"As my daughter, you're irreplaceable," her mom smiled, "but as a soda fountain clerk, I could easily hire a part-timer to fill your spot and probably have to pay them a lot less." She stepped forward and grabbed hold of Deanna's arms. "It used to be only Evan Colter who put that kind of sparkle in your eye, but when you just told me about your plans, you almost levitated off the seat. It does my heart good to see you excited about something. Lately, you've lost your pizzazz for life. I was starting to worry."

Whatever dam held her tears at bay burst, and Deanna

threw her arms around her mother. She sobbed for a good minute before she was able to talk. "I was scared the idea would make you unhappy."

"Don't be ridiculous." She patted Deanna's back. "What kind of mother would I be if I didn't want you to find joy in doing what you love?" She pushed her daughter away. "Now clean up your face, and let's get a move on."

Deanna swiped the moisture from her cheeks. "B-but you don't have to go with me. I'm not afraid to meet Mr. Amador alone."

"It's not about being afraid. I've known Tony since grade school. I dare him to refuse my baby girl a loan. And if he tries, I'll offer to cosign and put the museum up as collateral."

A second wave of tears hit. "Awww, Mama." She embraced her mother again. "You'd really do that?"

"On one condition." Her mother held her at arm's length. "The first wedding reception you hold in that spiffy new banquet hall better be your own. I'm sick of hearing all my friends brag about how cute their grandkids are."

Deanna laughed. "Deal. But you'll have to help me talk Evan into it."

EVAN BALANCED NEAR THE CHIMNEY AND POUNDED ANOTHER NAIL into the wooden shingle. This model was pricier than asphalt shingles, but it should give the ranch more of a rustic, homey appearance. He wanted any young man who arrived to get an impression of warmth and stability from the first moment he laid eyes on the spread.

He observed his first protégé. Marco had actually deigned to help today, probably because the job involved perching on the roof. Evan had been sure to get permission from his aunt when she dropped him off after school.

"Hey, Marco. Can you climb down the ladder and get me another package of shingles?"

The teen silently complied. He hadn't said a word from the time he'd arrived, but he followed directions well.

When Marco returned, Evan asked him to hold the shingles in place while he hammered. Truth be told, Evan didn't need help. It took longer teaching someone the ropes as they went along, but this project wasn't just about fixing the roof. A more important goal was drawing Marco out of his apathetic shell.

Evan's phone rang. He switched the hammer to his other hand, slipped the cell from a pocket on his leather tool belt, and answered. His conversation with Deanna took less than thirty seconds, most of which was spent listening as she spilled her jubilation about negotiating a loan to buy the old theater. When he suggested they meet for dinner to celebrate, her acceptance was almost as ardent as her excitement about the loan. They finished the conversation with a promise to meet later, and he hung up.

Marco passed him another shingle, and they got back to work. Memories of his own time at a boys' ranch flooded Evan's mind. He hadn't been much more communicative than Marco, but Pop Wilson drew him out, mostly by keeping up a steady stream of conversation whether Evan responded or not.

It was worth a shot.

"This type of shingle is twice as expensive as the common kind,"—he held one up—"but it looks more fitting on a Texas ranch than the boring, gray asphalt color. Don't you think?"

Marco chewed on his lime-green gum in response.

"I want this place to possess an old-timey feel, like something out of a John Wayne western. You've probably never seen one of those."

More silence.

Evan persevered. "I debated about what color to paint the barn. Red is the obvious choice, but that screams farm, not ranch. Would you agree?"

Marco shrugged.

Still, it was a response.

"Forest green was the right choice. Deanna liked the color so much, she wore it home."

The teen snickered. It would have been hard to miss how much paint Evan's enthusiastic fake fiancée had spilled on her overalls when she'd come to help.

Evan held a nail to the wood and tapped it with the hammer. "While she was here, Deanna got the great idea of offering ballroom dance classes to the guys who come to live on the ranch. And it's only fair to warn you,"—he held out his hand, and Marco passed him another shingle—"she mentioned practicing with you." He glanced up.

Marco's tilted head and wide eyes telegraphed his opinion loud and clear.

"Yeah, I figured you wouldn't be interested. There aren't many fourteen-year-olds these days who want to learn the waltz." Evan crawled to the left and started on a new line. "But you might prefer her other suggestion. Judo lessons."

Although Marco remained aloof, a spark of interest lit his face.

Evan slipped the hammer in the loop on the side of the tool belt. "Does that sound more enticing?"

His helper made a noise. If Evan interpreted the grunt correctly, it was a positive reaction.

He laughed quietly to himself. One thing was certain about Deanna Day, she knew how to capture a guy's attention, no matter the age.

A dust storm at the front entrance alerted them Renae was

back. The outspoken aunt drove her tiny coupe like she was qualifying for the next Grand Prix. She tore down the drive, screeched to a stop in front of the house, and exited the car in skin-tight jeans, an even tighter crop top, and red high heels.

Evan motioned to the ladder. "Let's wrap it up for the day."

They descended to the ground and joined Renae.

"How did it go?" she asked.

Evan waited for the teen to reply, but it appeared he didn't talk to anyone, including his own family.

"Not bad," Evan said. "With Marco's help, I got half the roof done."

She smirked. "Good thing he didn't fall off the house. His mom might have been peeved at me." Despite her sarcastic words, she wrapped an arm around her nephew. "It's nice to see you doing something productive."

Marco rolled his eyes but remained in her grasp.

Renae squeezed once and released him. "Why don't you wait for me in the car? I want to ask Mr. Colter something." Once the teen was out of earshot, she turned to Evan. "You're sure he's not bothering you?"

"We're good. The reason I'm preparing the ranch is for kids like him."

"More power to you." She shook her shoulders. "I couldn't stomach that much attitude."

"He started coming around a little bit today. I mentioned Deanna possibly giving him judo lessons, and it piqued his curiosity."

She laughed. "It's about time someone put him in his place. But I'm not sure Deanna is big enough to do it."

"Trust me,"—Evan rubbed his spine—"she gave a demonstration of how skilled she is. My back's still sore."

Renae studied him from head to toe before speaking. "You wouldn't be the first man to fall for little Miss Day's charms.

Although most of them don't actually end up flat on the ground."

The topic irked him, but he didn't want to analyze why. "As long as it's okay with Marco's mom, I'll have Deanna give him a lesson when he comes next week." He gestured at the car where the boy sat slumped on the front seat, hypnotized by his cell phone.

"I'm sure she won't care, but I'll ask anyway." Renae swayed to her coupe, opened the driver's side door, and looked at Evan over the roof of the car. "And don't think I missed how you changed the subject just now. If you ever decide not to join Deanna's long list of admirers, give me a call." She winked. "I'm sure we can find something fun to do." She climbed in before he could answer and drove away.

Long list?

Evan huffed. Exactly how many names were on this roster? He couldn't ask Deanna even though he knew she'd be honest. It might lead her to misunderstand his intentions as personal interest. It wasn't. He was watching out for her like an older brother protecting his sister.

But no matter how many men claimed to have dated Deanna, one thing was for sure. She'd only kissed him.

Chapter Twenty-Three

Grasping a small ring of keys, Deanna stood outside the theater's entrance. She'd signed the mortgage papers two days ago, but it still didn't feel real. She was an honest-to-goodness business owner.

"Nervous?" Evan stuck his head over her shoulder, close enough that his beard tickled her cheek.

"I'd be lying if I said no." She drew a wavery breath. "This is the biggest thing I've ever attempted. What if I fail?"

"Deanna Day? Fail?" He laid a hand on her arm and squeezed. "Impossible." With that same hand, he propelled her forward. "Now let's get started. You've been helping me at the ranch all week, so it's time I returned the favor."

"At least Marco decided to pitch in on the days his aunt dropped him off. Have you heard him say anything yet?"

Evan snorted. "Not a word. But you talk enough for the both of you."

"Somebody has to fill the silence. I've schooled him on the best classic movies, who were the most talented crooners of the golden age of Hollywood, and what kind of clothes are always in style, no matter the decade."

"I'm sure he'll get a lot of use from that pertinent information," Evan said with a straight face.

Deanna elbowed him in the gut. "How about we get to work?"

"Fine with me. But I've got to leave when it gets dark. I still have things to buy for the ranch before the stores close."

They entered the building and crossed the small lobby. Deanna and Evan each took an auditorium door, swung them wide, and propped them open with a couple of battered trash cans. The middle aisle stretched in front of them. Threadbare carpet with bulges and bald spots lined the walkway. It covered the slanted floor all the way to the orchestra pit.

Deanna flipped the cracked plastic switch on the wall, and light flooded the room. "Glad I called the electric company, or we'd be stumbling in the dark."

They walked past rows of busted theater seating. Cushions were torn from the backs. Splintered wood hung from the metal legs.

Evan retrieved a moldy velvet armrest from the floor. "I'm assuming some of the local miscreants hung out here. There's not much left in one piece."

"What was I thinking?" Deanna kicked at a piece of cushion stuffing lying on the floor. "Was I crazy to take this on? How in the world can I restore this place? I know nothing about building or carpentry or plumbing or—or—" She groaned. "I don't even know the right words to describe the stuff I'm ignorant about."

Evan chuckled. "Guess it's a good thing you've got a fake fiancé who spent twelve years in construction."

"But you're busy enough renovating the ranch. You don't have time to hold my hand through this project."

"It's true I'm busy, but"—he grabbed her right hand, raised

it, and peered at her fingers—"I can hold it awhile. For old times' sake."

Her lower lip jutted out. "You're too good to be true, Evan Colter. Even with both of us working, it will take weeks just to rip these decrepit old chairs out of the floor. We're in big trouble."

"Never fear." A strident voice sounded behind them. "The cavalry is here."

Lanette Johnson strode through the open doors. She wore a white sweatshirt with a hot pink flamingo painted on the left side. Rhinestones sparkled along the pockets of her jeans, and the laces of her tennis shoes perfectly matched the flamboyant bird on her chest. She marched down the aisle, drawing a pair of painter's gloves over her pristine manicure. Half a dozen men and women followed, carrying ladders, buckets, paintbrushes, and cleaning tools.

Lanette stopped beside the couple and wrapped an arm around Deanna. "Hello, lovebirds. You didn't think we'd make you fix this place up alone, did you?" She thumbed her finger in Evan's direction. "He can't stand the sight of me, but I figured even your greatest enemy is welcome on a thankless task like this."

"Hey, Lanette." Willy Walker approached with his ball cap turned backward. "Where should we start?"

"Deanna said something about chairs. Let's get these nasty, old seats out of the way. You and Harry can load them in your truck and take them to the dump."

"Got it." He pulled a wrench from his back pocket, knelt by a nearby row, and unscrewed a bolt from the floor.

Lanette gestured at the massive room. "This place is huge. We thought you two could use a little help."

"How did you find out we'd be working here?" Evan asked.

Lanette quirked an eyebrow. "You're kidding, right? I know

you've been gone a spell, but you must remember how this town works. If something happens at sunrise, everybody in town has heard before the bacon's finished frying."

"Be honest, Aunt Lanette." Deanna twisted in her hold. "Am I nuts for taking this on?"

"Maybe." She squeezed her tighter. "But it's the good kind of nuts. This world needs more crazy people like you."

Deanna blinked away the tears. "I don't deserve all these generous people in my life."

"Dry up the waterworks, sugar." Lanette slapped Deanna on the shoulder. "We've got work to do." She slapped Evan's shoulder next. "You two make a list of the problem areas, and we'll knock out as much as we can before sunset." The authoritative woman strode to the lobby, shouting an order at her husband as she went.

Evan shook his head. "She's gotten bossier over the years."

Deanna frowned. "Don't you say one bad word about Aunt Lanette. She'd give either one of us the flamingo shirt off her back." She towed him toward the door. "Let's do a quick walk-through and make that list. You've got the background in construction, so lend me your expertise. Might as well take advantage of this free help while we have the chance."

MORE TOWNSFOLK, INCLUDING AN EXTREMELY PEEVED BOONE Richardson, arrived to offer assistance as the day progressed. Evan worked with a few of the men, detaching the auditorium seats and carrying them outside. Others gathered the years of rubbish hidden in miscellaneous nooks and crannies and piled it in the lobby until it could be carted away.

After four hours of nonstop toil, Evan wandered into the lobby. Many helpers had left for lunch. The last time he'd seen

Deanna was when she and Lanette headed upstairs to start cleaning out the balcony.

Evan stared at the curved staircase on the side. Should he ask Deanna if she wanted some food? He chose the steps on the left and made it halfway up when he heard Boone's cajoling voice.

"You've been working too hard. Why not take a break and let me buy you lunch?"

"No thanks." Deanna's sweet but firm voice carried from the balcony. "I'll eat with my fiancé when he's ready."

Evan grinned. She was milking this fake engagement for all it was worth. He couldn't blame her for wanting to get rid of Richardson. The man was a pest. But it sounded like Deanna had everything under control, and his presence might add to the awkwardness. Evan returned to the lobby. It was better to give her rejected suitor a chance to escape without the embarrassment of being overheard.

Boone appeared on the landing. Evan and he met eyes, and the cowboy stomped down the stairs, the heels of his boots smacking the tiles with the force of a pile driver.

He thundered to where Evan stood. "Haven't you got enough to do without hanging around here?"

"I'm pretty busy remodeling the ranch lately. But Deanna has been a godsend, and I owe her a favor."

A muscle in Boone's jaw twitched at the revelation. "I don't know what you're up to, pal, but I'm watching you. You'd better not be using Deanna. She's got a soft heart, and she's always the first to help a charity case."

Charity case? Evan had to hand it to the man. He was good at getting someone's dander up. Evan took a slow breath before answering. "I would never do anything to hurt Deanna."

"Your very existence hurts her. The old hens in this town are having a field day gossiping about your supposed engagement. It ain't doing her reputation any good hanging around with you."

"Careful, Richardson," Evan ground out.

"Truth hurts, doesn't it?" The cowboy widened his stance and planted his hands on his jean-clad hips. "Your ancestor's statue may stand in the square on Main Street. But everyone in town remembers your father, and there's a reason they invented the old cliché: Like father, like son."

Evan remained silent. Boone had enough to say for both of them.

The man listed the crimes Evan's father had committed like he was reading a laundry list. "How can you ask Deanna to marry into a family with that kind of history?" Boone's eyes glinted. "I know you bought your old ranch. Are you trying to whitewash the Colter name? Maybe even follow in your daddy's footsteps and run for mayor?"

Evan didn't move. Didn't flinch. Didn't so much as clench his teeth. He hated the unfounded vitriol spewing from Richardson's mouth. But how could Evan respond? The man had justification for his accusations. Why would anyone trust the Colter name after what Evan's father did?

"Got nothin' to say?" Boone thrust his chin forward. "It's 'cause you can't deny it. Right? You think you're fooling people with your do-gooder act, but we're all wise to what you really want. To sit out on your"—he waggled his head—"*historic* ranch and reclaim the Colter dynasty."

Evan took a purposeful step backward. No matter how badly he wanted to flatten this idiot, he wouldn't give in to the baiting. But his heart pounded in direct defiance of his self-control.

Splash!

A torrent of water crashed onto Boone's head. It gushed onto the hard-tiled floor and doused Evan's pant legs. He jumped away. Both men looked up. Deanna's head poked over the railing of the landing outside the balcony door, an empty bucket in her hand.

"Boone Richardson," she bellowed, "I'm ashamed of you." She tossed the bucket on the ground, careened down the stairs, and stood between the two of them, directing her fury at the surly, wet cowboy. "How can you treat Evan this way? We all went to school together. We've been friends for years."

"He ain't no friend of mine," grumbled Boone. "Even back in school, he always acted better than us."

"That's just your own insecurity talking. Evan has had a hard enough time returning to Sweetheart without you confirming for him that there are still prejudiced, mealy-mouthed bigots living here. He didn't buy the Double Heart Ranch for himself. He's transforming it into a rehabilitation center for troubled youth."

"Oh great." Boone stuck his arms in the air, fingers spread wide. "He's importing delinquents into our peaceful town. That's even worse."

Deanna poked him. "You ought to be thanking him for helping kids turn their lives around." Another poke. "Any decent human being would feel proud to be a part of his plan."

"De-aaaa-na." The cowboy's tone wheedled from his lips. "You and me have been getting to know each other real well lately. How can you take the side of someone who hasn't so much as sent you a postcard in the past twenty years?"

"It's only natural a girl defends the man she loves."

Loves?

Evan's heart pounded for an entirely new reason. He was listening to the barrage of hate and prejudice he'd feared he would find in Sweetheart. But now that he was facing it head-on, it didn't seem that bad, because of the tiny, blonde wonder in front of him. His pint-size protector balled her fists like she'd flatten Boone Richardson if he took a step in their direction.

Boone's lower lip protruded. He sniffed and stalked away, leaving the two of them alone in the hallway.

Deanna rounded on Evan. "Did you forget how to talk? Why did you stand there and take that kind of guff?"

He rubbed his beard. "It's hard to argue with the truth. My dad really did all the things Richardson accused him of."

"But *you* didn't." Apparently, Deanna wasn't done poking. She jabbed her finger into Evan's belly. "When are you going to stop blaming yourself for what your father did wrong? Yes, a few fools like Boone Richardson will dredge up the past, but there are plenty of intelligent people in Sweetheart who don't hold it against you. You need to start speaking up for yourself. Got it?"

Evan gave a soft laugh. "Yes, ma'am. And thank you for riding in to save the day."

Deanna smiled before heaving a dramatic sigh. "I sure wish somebody would realize how hungry I am. It's been hours since breakfast."

"Forgive me, dear fiancée." Evan offered his arm with a flourish. "Your wish is my command. Whatever you desire."

Her eyebrows rose. "That's a dangerous offer to make a smitten girl. You might find yourself in front of the preacher."

Evan laughed even louder. She was joking, of course, but one thing was for sure. The man who married Deanna Day would have a true-blue, devoted champion on his side for life.

Chapter Twenty-Four

Deanna pushed the pedals of her bicycle down the long ranch driveway. Her teeth rattled as she bounced along the dented road. She'd changed her clothes after church because a thick crinoline would not have fared well on the thirty-minute trip. Since Evan had moved out to the ranch, there was no need to visit the gym. Perhaps she should consider purchasing an electric scooter. Or a moped. Her legs burned from the exertion. She pulled up to the house, hobbled off the bike, and rubbed her left calf.

"Are you okay?" Evan exited the house with two small bottles of soda.

"I'm probably the healthiest I've ever been. Between working at the theater and pedaling out here multiple times a week, my muscles don't know what to do with all this exercise."

"I'll give you a ride home later. We can load your bike in the back of my truck." He eyed her vintage Streamliner with disdain. "Remind me to give you that driving lesson you keep putting off."

"No thanks." Deanna popped the kickstand. "The truth is, I

abandoned those ages ago. I've accepted I don't have a talent for driving. Where's Marco?"

Evan lifted one finger off the soda bottle and pointed to the barn, where the young man was walking out with an armload of wood. "We're making good progress. I've told him it won't be too long before the little jobs he can help with are done. That must have made him happy."

Deanna waved at the teen, who gave no response. He approached them without a word.

Evan nodded at the porch. "Dump everything there and take a break, Marco. When you're ready, Deanna can give you a judo lesson." He gave one of the sodas to the boy and offered the other to Deanna.

"I'd better not," she said. "Too much caffeine doesn't work well with my metabolism—makes me jittery. And I'm afraid I can only stay a little while. There's a rehearsal tonight for the Sweet Shakes program next weekend."

Evan rolled the plastic bottle between his hands. "Will Boone be there?"

"He'd better be. He's Romeo." Deanna stretched to the sky. "What a beautiful day!" She stopped and squinted at a thin wisp of smoke drifting above the roof. "What's that? Is something on fire?"

Evan bolted around the house, Deanna and Marco at his heels. They rounded the corner, and a small crop of flames was visible by the back fence. It burned along the grass, blackening the new wooden posts they'd painted yesterday.

"Get the hose!" Evan dropped the bottle, approached one end of the short blaze, and stomped on it with his boot.

Marco dashed to the garden, grabbed the hose, and hurried to the spigot.

Deanna spun in a panicked circle. How could she help? Her gaze jerked from one side to the other. Spying a bucket with soil near the planter boxes, she grabbed it, ran to the fire, and dumped the contents on the opposite end of the blaze from where Evan was stomping. It helped, but not much.

Marco returned with the hose and pointed the water at the flames. They lessened under the strong spray.

An idea hit Deanna. She grabbed the discarded drink bottle from the grass and twisted off the cap. Plugging the hole with her thumb, she shook the soda like crazy, then aimed the top at the remaining flames. The carbonated mix shot out in a fizzy explosion. The fire died in an instant.

"Whoa," said Marco.

"You talked!" Deanna dropped the empty bottle and covered her mouth. "Oh my word. Evan, did you hear? Marco said something."

Evan nodded. "One whole word. Your eloquence is breathtaking, Marco."

The kid grinned in response.

"Great work." Deanna pounded him on the back. "You put out most of the flames with the hose. You're a hero."

"To be fair, you both played a part." Evan retrieved the empty soda bottle and held it up. "That was a neat trick, Deanna. Where'd you learn it?"

"I saw it on social media."

Marco guffawed at her revelation.

"What?" Deanna faked a pout. "You're not the only one with a cell phone, mister. I watch viral videos too."

Evan left them to examine the charred remains of grass. He knelt and pushed against the bottom of a fence post. It splintered at the force he applied.

"Is it bad?" Deanna joined him.

"Not really. But this post will have to be replaced."

She drew close to peer over his shoulder. "What caused the fire in the first place?"

"I don't know." He poked at the ground. "It's been dry lately. Not much rain. Could have been some sort of chemical reaction."

"What a shame. Y'all just finished the fence yesterday."

Evan straightened. "At least it's a small section. Marco can help me replace it tomorrow. Oh, wait." He looked at the teen. "Tomorrow's Monday. I'll have to fix it myself."

Marco shrugged. "My aunt can drop me off after school if you want to wait."

Deanna and Evan stared. They'd never heard a full sentence from the young man. The fact that it was an offer of assistance made it doubly astonishing.

Evan pressed his lips together. "Sounds good." He knelt at another section of the fence.

Marco wandered away, pulling his phone from his back pocket.

Deanna rolled her eyes. She wanted to gather them both in a group hug at this momentous emotional breakthrough, but Evan and Marco were carrying on as if it were no big deal.

Men.

EVAN SAT BESIDE MARCO ON THE PORCH STEPS. THE TEEN HADN'T spoken another word the whole day, no matter how Deanna tried to engage him in conversation. The most noise he made was grunting when she taught him the proper martial arts way to fall, which looked more like the two of them doing somersaults on a hay pile. Undeterred, she'd grabbed him in a bear hug before pedaling away on her ridiculous bicycle.

If Marco was already gone, Evan would have given her a ride, but he had to wait until Renae arrived. Even though this was the safe, small town of Sweetheart, he hated the idea of her biking thirty minutes alone each way. It was high time Deanna learned to drive. He should insist on a lesson the next time she was out at the ranch.

Marco shifted and chewed his ever-present gum.

Evan turned his face the teen's way. "Thanks for offering to come tomorrow."

"No big deal."

Three whole words. Even the charming Deanna hadn't been able to coax that much out of Marco.

Evan stretched his legs out and crossed his ankles. "Do you need me to come get you?"

"I'll ride my bike."

"Does everyone in Sweetheart own bicycles? You and Deanna could form a club."

Marco scoffed. "Yeah, right."

"I'm planning to teach her to drive. Someday, when you get your permit, I can teach you too. If it's okay with your mom."

A flash of excitement crossed Marco's face, but he quickly hid it. "That'd be okay."

"Good."

A comforting sense of purpose filled Evan's soul. He'd drifted for so many years. Working construction jobs to make money, yet lacking any real passion or calling. But this felt right. Building a true connection with Marco proved he could also help others.

Just as his great-great-grandfather had driven a stake in the ground that would one day grow into the thriving town of Sweetheart, Evan could build a community of his own. A place where those without a home belonged.

And maybe.

If he tried really hard.

He could find that home, too.

Chapter Twenty-Five

runch. Crunch. Crunch.

Hay crackled underneath Deanna's feet as she led Marco to their pretend arena. After the fence post was fixed, Evan had spread three bales across the grass by the barn to ensure they had plenty of padding for their judo lesson. Today, she was planning to teach Marco a few throws. They practiced in the yard while Evan, wearing jeans and a red flannel shirt that made him look like the model from a wilderness ad, painted the slats on the front porch.

After Deanna demonstrated a simple throw, laughter startled her.

Marco lay on his back with a huge smile. Hay stuck from his curly hair. He wore the white judo outfit she'd brought for him to keep. It matched hers exactly, except for the color of their belts. Hers was black. His was white.

"What's the matter?" Deanna made a face at him. "Are you going to let a girl beat you?"

"You're not a girl." He hopped up.

Deanna forced herself not to react. She'd heard Marco speaking more to Evan, but this was the first time with her. She propped her hands on her hips. "I'm not a girl? Then what am I?"

He squatted with his arms raised in attack mode. "An old lady." The playful bounce of his eyebrows lessened the severity of the words.

Deanna squealed in mock horror. "Did you hear that, Evan?" She hollered toward the porch. "You'd better marry me before the kids in this town start calling me a spinster."

Evan didn't answer. Didn't even acknowledge her.

Marco laughed again. "Or grandma."

"That's it, buddy. You're going down." She grabbed one of Marco's arms, inserted a foot behind his, and gently tossed him over her leg. She helped him up, then lifted her left arm. "Now, you try. Grip my sleeve. That's right."

She coached the teen through the steps until she was the one sprawled on the hay. The two practiced the move for the next fifteen minutes. The exertion made her heart pound like the bass drum in a marching band. With the unlimited energy of youth, Marco spun ninja-style and landed spread-eagled a foot away. She collapsed on the ground, her chest heaving.

Deanna gasped. "I'm out of practice."

Evan walked by them, rinsed out his brush at a spigot on the side of the barn, and left it on a crate to dry. "That's enough, you two. Marco may be fourteen, but some people are in their thirties here. You'd better take a rest, Deanna." He joined them at the edge of the hay mat.

She stood and dusted the dirt from her pant leg. "May I remind a certain man in his thirties that he's seven whole hours older than me?"

"That's right." Evan nodded. "And as an older brother, it's my job to look out for you."

Older brother? Deanna squinted. They'd crashed through that barrier long ago.

Her chin jutted. "I'm an only child. I don't have any siblings."

Marco's brow puckered. "Aren't you two getting married? Aunt Renae was complaining about it last night. Said you should marry that Richardson guy instead."

A glint entered Deanna's eyes. "You tell your Aunt Renae that Boone is just a friend."

"A friend you're playing Romeo and Juliet with." Evan's voice was a little too casual. "How did rehearsal go?"

"Not bad." Was he asking because he was jealous? "Boone's improved since last year. I may finally get my tragic death scene. This time, I want to make people weep instead of laugh. But we still need a few extras for the Julius Caesar murder scene. Interested?"

Evan's response was to cross his arms.

Deanna turned to the teen beside them. "What do you say, Marco? Have you ever fancied being onstage? You'd even wear a toga."

The absolute horror on his face said it all. He spat his lime-green gum into the hay.

"Fine. No toga." She poked a finger at Evan's biceps. "But you two can still play audience members, right?"

"I'm not into Shakespeare." Marco wandered to stand beside Evan and copied his uninviting stance.

"Me either," said Evan.

"Okay." Deanna adjusted the belt on her uniform. "Fine. There will be plenty of other people there. I'll ask Boone to drive me home when it's over. After him squeezing into a pair of tights for two years in a row, just to please me, I should probably cook the poor man dinner as a thank-you."

"I don't think food poisoning is the best way to thank someone," Evan said.

Marco snickered.

Deanna lifted her nose. "*Some* men will eat everything I cook without complaining."

Evan's lips twitched. "There's no fixing stupid." He held up both hands. "But I guess I owe it to my old classmate Boone to save him a bellyache. He can take his time peeling off the tights, and I'll drive you home after the festivities. You might even talk me into buying you some of Willy Walker's famous moist brisket."

"Brisket?" Marco stood straighter. "Can I come too?"

Deanna eyed him. "I thought Shakespeare wasn't your thing."

"It's not"—the teen smirked—"but barbecue is."

"Of course you're invited." Evan clapped him on the back. "You've given me more help than a whole crew. Before you know it, all the big stuff will be done and your aunt won't make you come over so much."

A serious expression replaced Marco's smile. The muscle in his jaw protruded as he looked away. "About time."

Deanna tapped his shoulder. "Since you're going to be at the show anyway, it's not too late for me to find you a toga. You'd get to pretend-stab someone with a pool noodle."

Marco jerked away from her touch and stalked off while muttering, "I need a drink."

Deanna stared after the moody young man. He'd been open during the judo lesson, even laughing and joking around. What flipped the switch?

She tugged on Evan's flannel sleeve. "Did I say the wrong thing?"

He shrugged. "With teenagers, it doesn't take much. Give him space, and he'll come around."

Deanna's lips lifted.

"What?" Evan squirmed under her perusal.

"You're good with Marco. I can see why you wanted to convert the ranch to help boys like him."

Evan kicked at the hay on the ground. "It's because I can relate."

"No, it's more than that. You have a God-given wisdom when it comes to talking with Marco. Did you study psychology in college?"

"I didn't go to college." Evan walked away and grabbed the paintbrush from the crate. He strode through the side door of the barn.

Deanna followed him into the cool, dusty interior. "That surprises me." She walked to where Evan stood by a worktable along the nearby wall. "You were always the number one student in our class."

"Yeah, well. That was a long time ago." He shook the brush forcefully, and a few drops of water splattered her.

Deanna reared back.

"Sorry." Evan dropped the paintbrush, pulled the cuff of his sleeve over his hand, and dabbed at her cheek.

The soft, red material caressed Deanna's skin. She tried to make eye contact, but Evan avoided it. "Did I hit a sore spot? I didn't mean to."

His gaze met hers. "It's not you. I'm a bit defensive about the college thing. My mom pushed me to get a degree, but even after my time at the ranch straightened me out, I still had issues." He lowered his hand. "Not legal issues, but I spent quite a few years looking for a good time. Did some things I'm not proud of." His chin tilted like he was bracing himself for her disappointment.

Deanna wrapped her arms tight around his waist and pressed her cheek to his torso. "I'm sorry you don't have more happy memories."

His tense body relaxed. "I just wish I hadn't wasted so long wandering from city to city, working odd jobs in construction to pay the bills. I could have done more."

She leaned back. "But then you wouldn't have learned the multitude of skills you needed to fix up this ranch. Isn't it amazing how God never lets anything go to waste, even the things we label 'bad stuff'?"

Evan's brows lifted in a sarcastic arc, but he didn't reply.

"Besides,"—Deanna swatted his chest—"it's not too late. There are such things as online courses. You can get your degree from the comfort of your own living room."

Evan laughed. "You sound like a commercial."

"At least consider it. I bet you'd be good at psychology. Or maybe counseling."

"You think so?"

"Absolutely. You already possess a natural talent for connecting with people. Look how you've drawn Marco out of his shell. You're practically an expert."

"Speaking of Marco, I'd better check on him." Evan strode to the wide-open front doors. "And if you'd allow an expert's advice, I suggest you don't mention togas this time."

"Spoilsport," Deanna called after him.

They exited the barn and saw Marco sitting on the front porch steps, drinking a soda.

"Hey, Marco," Evan hollered. "We're finished for the day. I'll take you and Deanna home."

The teen dragged himself to a standing position and waited. Together, the three of them walked to the side of the house where Evan had parked his truck. Deanna moved to the passenger side and was about to open the door when something stopped her.

"Uh-oh."

"What's the problem?" Evan hurried around the truck's bed.

She pointed at the front wheel. The bottom part of the tire squished flat against the grass. They weren't going anywhere.

"Great," Evan moaned. "One more thing to fix."

"Do you have a spare?"

"Of course. And I've got even better." Evan crossed to where Marco hovered near the tailgate and threw his arm around the boy's shoulders. "I've got a smart, strong assistant. With Marco's help, we'll fix that flat in no time."

The teen grinned for a split second before schooling his features into their regular impassive mask. Evan left to fetch a jack from the barn, and Marco scampered after him, copying everything from the older man's posture to his stride. Deanna chuckled at the sight.

It appeared God brought Evan Colter back to Sweetheart for more than just her sake. Good thing she wasn't the possessive type.

Chapter Twenty-Six

"To be or not to be. That shore is the question."

Evan wondered how he'd lived for thirty-three years without hearing Hamlet's famous soliloquy in a thick Southern-Texas accent. The park was filled with locals and out-of-towners on camp chairs and picnic blankets. A few people slung the blankets around their bodies as the night temperatures dropped.

Willy Walker stood on the gazebo stage in a velvet costume. A long quill feather drooped from his lopsided hat as he added his own flair to each famous line.

Laughter bubbled from the crowd at his unique interpretation of the Bard. It added to the humor that the man held an old cattle skull with horns instead of the human kind traditionally used. Yes. Sweetheart's tribute to Shakespeare was one for the history books.

Willy concluded the scene to thunderous applause, and the master of ceremonies announced a fifteen-minute intermission before the second half.

Marco stirred beside Evan. The teen had spent most of the

show playing a game on his phone. "I'm gonna buy a churro," he said before standing up and heading to the food stalls.

Evan rose from his seat and wandered to the curtained-off area in the back where the performers waited. Deanna might be hungry. Her act was the big finale. He heard her panicked voice as he drew near the white sheets strung between two oak trees.

"This is a disaster," she wailed.

Evan stopped at the curtains and leaned his head close. "Deanna, are you okay?"

Her hand reached through the two pieces of fabric and yanked him through. She was dressed in a floor-length burgundy gown with gaping, medieval-style sleeves that brushed the ground. Beside her stood Renae with an unconcerned smirk on her bright red lips. She scrolled through her phone as Deanna pressed her temples and moaned.

"No, I'm not okay," said Deanna. "When Boone was leaving his house, he stepped off the porch wrong and twisted his ankle. How can we perform *Romeo and Juliet* with no Romeo?"

"That would be challenging," Evan agreed.

Renae looked up from her cell and shrugged. "He wasn't much of a Romeo anyway. I had to keep feeding him his lines. What are we gonna do?"

"I don't know." Deanna chewed on her lower lip. "Boone didn't have an understudy. It's the death scene, so we could put his costume on the female mannequin we used for the King Lear scene with Cordelia." Her breath left her mouth in a noisy growl. "But that will totally take away from the romantic ambiance. If only we'd—" Her eyes widened, and her head jerked Evan's way. "Wait a minute! Evan, what size are you?"

He retreated. "I see where your brain is headed, and you can stop right there. I'm not wearing tights. Not even for you."

"Please, Evan. You have time to mentally prepare. The

death scene from *Julius Caesar* goes first." She advanced with hands outstretched. "Pretty, pretty please with all the sugar in the world on top. I've waited a year to have a second chance at *The Tragedy of Romeo and Juliet.* This is the big finale—a love worth dying for! The night won't end right if we close with a mob stabbing. We use pool noodles instead of knives, but it's still way too morbid. Can't you help us out?"

He folded his arms. "I don't know any of the lines. What am I supposed to do? Carry a cheat sheet in my lace cuff?"

"We'll just start the scene later when Romeo is already dead, and we're both lying there. I'll awake and do all the talking." She laid a hand on his chest and stared up at him. "Please? You don't even have to wear the tights. The poet blouse over a pair of black dress slacks will do."

Evan shook his head without a word.

Deanna's lower lip trembled, and she pushed him away. "Fine. Abandon me. I don't need you. I'll quote my lines to the mannequin."

"I like it." Renae laughed. "I bet the dummy will still have more personality than Boone did in rehearsal."

Evan nodded. "You were playing this night for comedy anyway, right? I think it will work."

Moisture welled in Deanna's eyes. The sight made Evan's stomach drop. He reached for her, but she pulled away and glared at him through her tears.

"There's comedy, and then there's ridiculous. I'll probably be the laughingstock of the whole town. They'll talk about this for months. Again." She swiped at her wet lashes. "But I'm a professional, so I have no choice. The show must go on." She flounced away with her nose in the air.

Renae snorted. "No wonder she loves the stage. It gives her an audience for all that drama." She bared her teeth in Evan's direction. "You aren't really gonna let her go out there alone, are you? All you have to do is lie there and play dead."

He rubbed his face and sighed. "I refuse to wear the tights."

"No problem." Renae spun and chose a billowy, white dress shirt from the rack. "Pick whatever pants you like." She cocked her head and studied him. "But the mountain man hermit look has got to go."

"What do you mean?"

"Romeo is supposed to be a sixteen-year-old kid. You're way past puberty, but it'll be easier for the audience to suspend disbelief if you shave." She snagged an electric razor from the table and walked toward him.

"Whoa." Evan held up both hands. "Don't touch the beard. I'm just going to be lying there like a fancy corpse. What does it matter if I have facial hair?"

"It matters to Deanna." She gave him the once-over. "It's either a shave or the tights."

Evan gulped. Why was he even considering this? Deanna must have hypnotized him with her tears. He wanted to turn tail and run, but the thought of disappointing her drilled a hole in his gut. She'd been the first to welcome him back to Sweetheart. And she'd stood by him no matter how tense or embarrassing the situation. He couldn't let her down now.

He fingered the hairs on his cheek. "My face will feel naked without it."

Renae pressed the button on the razor. It buzzed, and she smiled. "You can grow it back."

Chapter Twenty-
Seven

W hat was with men and their aversion to tights?
Deanna tried to recruit another Romeo during
the last five minutes of Julius Caesar's death by
pool noodles, but Evan's dislike of the costume
seemed to be contagious. Every male she asked stared at her in
disbelief before hightailing it faster than a hot rod.

She slipped behind the curtained-off dressing area and
found Renae dusting something from a stool.

Deanna approached her with clenched teeth. "Bad news,
Renae. No one will take Boone's place. We're stuck with the
dummy."

Renae snickered but made no reply.

Deanna picked up her beaded pearl headdress, settled it on
her hair, and took one last glance in the mirror. "Can you carry
it onstage after I spread my dress out on the funeral pier?"

"Don't worry." Renae smirked. "I'll make sure the right
dummy gets out there."

Laughter and cheers erupted from the audience, letting
them know Brutus and his buddies were taking their bows.
Deanna waited until the main curtain at the front of the

gazebo dropped, and then she wove past her fellow actors to take the stage. The men toted out the flower-adorned funeral pier, and she sat on top and arranged her velvet skirt before reclining and closing her eyes. At least she could look good while quoting some of the most romantic lines in all of literature to a plastic corpse.

Willy Walker's voice boomed from the other side of the curtain as he asked the audience if they were enjoying their Et Tu Brute Barbecue.

"Last year, it was a cupful of water straight in the kisser," Deanna mumbled to herself. "This year, it's no Romeo. Why can't I have one decent shot at this scene?"

Heavy footsteps entered from the side. Renae must be carrying out the dummy. The body settled beside her. It was bigger than she remembered. That was good. The audience might mistake it for a human being.

The MC announced the final scene, and the sound of the curtain being whisked away told Deanna it was showtime. She opened her eyes, feigned a yawn, and rose to a sitting position.

"What's here?" She spoke in her best British accent. Shakespeare always sounded better in jolly Old English. "A cup …"

She took it from the hand beside her, and her fingers brushed warm flesh. Her gaze flew to her Romeo. It wasn't a dummy. It was—Evan? Maybe.

The chiseled features of the handsome person resembled him, but the beard was gone. Oh my word, the man was exquisite. She already knew that, but the absence of facial hair multiplied his gorgeousness exponentially.

Deanna stared in awe.

Evan cracked one blue eye open and whispered, "Did you forget your line?"

"Oh! A—a cup," she raised the goblet, "closed in my true love's hand?"

He shut his eye and remained still.

Deanna regained her acting equilibrium and was determined to enjoy the scene now that she had a proper Romeo. "Poison, I see, hath been his timeless end." She pretended to drink from the cup and threw it to the side in disgust. "O churl, drunk all, and left no friendly drop to help me after?" She turned to Evan. "I will kiss thy lips; Haply some poison yet doth hang on them ..."

As she bent close, her pulse fluttered softly like a butterfly's wings. Without the beard, he was transformed. In his face, she found traces of the boy he used to be—the one who had filled her girlish dreams. She had more lines to quote, but couldn't remember the words. Leaning over Evan's chiseled jaw drove rational thought from her brain. A sudden and inexplicable wave of bashfulness hit her. How ridiculous. She'd kissed him multiple times since his return, but this cleaned-up version of Evan Colter rivaled Cary Grant, Gregory Peck, and Gene Kelly all rolled into one.

Deanna drew closer. The beat of her heart pounded in her ears. At the last second, she slipped her thumb on top of his mouth and laid a kiss on her own finger. "Thy lips are warm!"

Evan cracked a questioning eye once again. Deanna grabbed the fake dagger from the sheath at his side, made quick work of her final lines, and plunged the collapsible prop into her bodice. She fell across his chest in a fashionable heap, making sure her billowy sleeves fanned in an artful spill. A brief silence followed before applause sounded from the audience.

Deanna resurrected at lightning speed and grabbed Evan's lace-edged sleeve. "Come on. Let's take a bow."

They rose from the flower-bedecked pier. He stood beside

her at the front of the stage and gave an awkward half-bend at the waist. Deanna held the sides of her velvet costume and gave a full-blown curtsy. Then decided to steal a second one. Didn't she deserve it after all? Two years in a row, her glorious death scene had been stolen by unforeseen circumstances. This time hadn't been as disastrous as playing opposite a dummy, but her ambitions of losing herself in the grief and emotion of Juliet's death scene remained unfulfilled.

"Maybe next year," she muttered.

"What?" Evan cast a glance her way.

"Nothing."

They exited stage right. The other actors met them in the dressing area and offered congratulations on the successful finale. Deanna accepted them with aplomb before pulling Evan to the side for a whispered conversation.

"What happened? You categorically refused to play Romeo."

He gestured to his black slacks. "I refused to wear the tights, but"—he scrubbed his bare cheek, seemed shocked to find his beard gone, and dropped his hand in embarrassment —"but I couldn't let your play be ruined."

"Since when does the Sweet Shakes Weekend matter to you?"

"It matters to *you*." He shrugged. "That's a good enough reason."

Deanna's pique evaporated. He'd done it for her. Worn a ridiculous, frilly shirt and let her pretend sob all over him, just to make her happy. If she hadn't already been in love with him for three decades, she definitely would be now.

Evan quirked his head. "What was with the finger kiss?"

"Were you disappointed?" Deanna nudged him.

"Hardly." He tugged at the low-cut neckline of his costume.

"But earlier, you were champing at the bit for romantic ambiance."

"Trust me, Evan Colter. I'll be happy to repeat the scene with you as many times as you'll let me, complete with a real smooch at the end."

He chuckled. "With that much rehearsal, we should be pretty good by next year."

Next year?

The two words hit her with all the joyous serendipity of a surprise party. It confirmed they had a future together. That Evan saw them being close enough to do a kissing scene again, three hundred sixty-five days from now.

Another thought hit with the unwelcome shock of a tax audit. Would he feel differently if she ever admitted the unwitting part she'd played in his father's arrest?

Deanna sniffled. She turned away and brushed a long, velvet sleeve across her cheeks.

"What's wrong?" Evan asked.

"N-nothing. Something's in my eye." She swallowed her tears, met him with a beaming smile, and looped her arm around his. "Shaving and playing dead weren't part of your plans for this evening. I owe you a big favor. How can I repay you?"

He grew contemplative. "There *is* something you can do for me."

"Great!" She bounced on her heels. "Name it."

"Let me give you a driving lesson."

She yanked her arm away and took a step back. "Driving and I don't get along. And how exactly would that benefit you?"

"It grants me peace of mind. I hate how far you have to bike out to the Double Heart, but you keep refusing to let me pick you up."

"You're busy enough renovating the ranch." She twirled and walked to the nearby costume table, removing the beaded hat from her head. "Can't I pay my debt some other way?"

He crossed his arms. "Sorry. That's all I want."

Deanna tossed the hat on the table. "Come on, Colter. Let me off the hook."

"Sure." His grin was positively angelic. "After you take a lesson with me."

Willy Walker poked his head between the curtains. "Hey, Deanna, there's still barbecue left if y'all are hungry."

"Thanks, Willy." She waved at him and returned her attention to Evan. "Can't you think of any other payment you'll accept?"

He shook his head.

She covered her face and moaned. "Why couldn't I pick another Romeo?"

Chapter Twenty-Eight

Deanna shuddered at the steering wheel in front of her. The dreaded driving lesson arrived too fast. Never had a four-wheel drive truck appeared so scary. She looked to the right at Evan, who was typing on his phone. The sharp angle of his jaw drew her gaze. Her fingers itched to touch the now-smooth skin, but she stopped herself in time.

Must behave.

Must keep her hands to herself.

Better to concentrate on something besides his undeniable drop-deadness. Was that even a thing? There didn't seem to be a word magnificent enough to describe clean-shaven Evan Colter.

She lasted all of twenty seconds before sneaking another peek. His caramel-colored locks spilled onto his forehead like he hadn't bothered to do more than finger-comb them. Obviously, he hadn't spent as much time primping for their meetup as she had. Deanna readjusted the yellow checkered scarf she'd tied milkmaid style over her hair. It perfectly matched her white capri pants with a checkered, wraparound half skirt. She would usually be thrilled to spend the evening together, but this wasn't a romantic date night. A serious task awaited them—one she'd rather forget.

Deanna nibbled on her lip. "I have a confession to make."

The skin near Evan's eyes crinkled as he put his phone away. "Don't tell me you've recruited another fake fiancé."

"No. But I'm not exactly ecstatic about what we're doing. Truth be told, I'm shaking in my sandals."

"That's okay." He draped an arm along the back of the bench seat. "Most people find learning to drive scary. Then again, most people are teenagers when they attempt it."

"I attempted it," Deanna grumbled. "I just never finished."

"Then it's high time you do. Don't worry. I'll be right by your side, and we've got lots of room." He motioned past the windshield to the giant parking lot of the supermarket. "Hardly anyone is shopping tonight. We'll stick to the outer edges until you grow more comfortable, and then we can try a few back roads."

"Whoopee," Deanna said without an ounce of enthusiasm.

Evan pointed at the gearshift. "Put it in Drive and press your foot gently on the gas pedal."

"Not until I do one crucial thing." She clasped her hands together and peered through the windshield at the sky. "Dear Lord, please help me stay calm. Please make my brain remember everything. Please don't let me hurt anyone. Or Evan's truck—"

"Especially not Evan's truck," he chimed in.

"And please keep the other drivers and squirrels and trees out of my path."

"Amen."

"Look at you." Deanna grinned at him. "You're even talking to the Almighty now."

He shrugged. "When it comes to my truck, I'm willing to take all the help I can get."

She adjusted the gearshift, took hold of the steering wheel, and pressed a tentative foot to the pedal. Was it her imagination, or could she feel the engine roaring? The scary vibrations traveled through the rope sole of the authentic espadrille sandal she'd purchased in Mexico on her last vacation.

Deanna pressed harder. The truck jolted forward. She slammed the brakes. Her torso crashed against the seat belt and flopped back onto the bench.

"Sorry." She grimaced at Evan.

"No worries." He cracked his neck. "But press down a little easier next time."

She tried again, pushing her right foot slowly on the gas pedal. The vehicle crept forward.

Okay. This was doable. Not too scary. No violent movements. She pushed more. The truck jolted. She braked with her left foot.

Gas. Brake. Gas. Brake.

"Deanna," Evan croaked from beside her, "let's pause for a second."

She turned her head in a slow arc, afraid to look at him. He was rubbing the back of his head. Of course he was. She'd probably given him whiplash, and they'd been at it for a mere two minutes.

He somehow managed a smile. "I know driving this big truck is daunting. But it's not going anywhere you don't tell it to. When you put your foot on the gas or the brake, use the same amount of pressure as ..." He held up a finger. "You took piano lessons, right?"

"For ten long years."

"Use the same force you would on the piano pedal. Gently

compress the gas with your right foot, then use that same foot on the brake when you need to stop. The only time you would use both feet is when you're driving a stick shift."

"The right." Deanna nodded. "Got it."

She took a deep breath, shot a silent prayer to Heaven, and pressed the gas pedal with her right foot—ever so slowly. The truck inched forward. She drove in a straight line until they reached the end of the parking lot, then rotated the steering wheel until they headed in the opposite direction.

"Am I going too fast?" she squeaked.

"At eleven miles an hour?" Evan dryly replied. "I doubt the police will flag you down."

She noted the way the white-striped parking spots crawled by the window and dared to press her foot more forcefully. The engine revved, and she shrieked.

"Wow, eighteen miles an hour." Evan pumped a fist in the air. "We're breaking the sound barrier."

They made at least half a dozen snail-paced laps in the empty part of the lot before Deanna pressed the brake again. She rubbed her leg.

"What's the matter?" Evan asked. "Did you get a charley horse?"

"No. I chose the wrong driving shoes. These ribbon straps are biting into my ankle." She slipped a finger under the fabric and tugged to loosen it. "That's better." She straightened. "I'm not shaking anymore. In fact, I've worked up enough courage to venture out on the road."

"Perfect timing, since it's past Sweetheart's rush hour. I'd hate for you to get caught in a five-car traffic jam." He made a big show of tightening his seat belt and clutching the armrest. "Okay, I'm ready."

Deanna laughed and drove them out of the parking lot onto the road. She took a right at the Stop sign, and they made their way through a residential neighborhood. The houses were spaced far apart with wide yards surrounding them. No other cars appeared on the other side of the two-lane road, and Deanna's shoulders started to unwind.

"Has this truck got any good music?" she asked.

Evan withdrew his phone and checked the Bluetooth connection. "Any requests?"

"Do you even have to ask? It's November. Crank up the Christmas tunes."

A few seconds later, a rousing big band rendition of "Jingle Bells" played through the cab.

"That's more like it." Deanna tapped the foot that wasn't pressing the gas pedal.

The truck drifted slightly to the right, and Evan reached to grab the wheel. "Be sure to stay in your lane."

"Yes, sir." Deanna focused. She checked the speedometer. Thirty-six miles an hour. She'd better cut back before she got a ticket for speeding. The sandal on her right foot shifted, and she maneuvered her heel to settle it in place.

"How could you last this long without learning to drive?" Evan asked. "I'd go stir-crazy having to travel only within bike-riding distance. What did you do when the weather was bad?"

"This is Sweetheart. It usually doesn't get cold enough in the winter to make much difference. I bundled up in a jacket and scarf, and I was fine. And I had plenty of friends who gave me a ride if it was raining."

"Friends or dates?" His tone was peevish.

"Both," she gleefully retorted.

The houses grew less frequent. Fenced-in pastureland stretched on both sides of the road. They didn't speak for a while, but the silence was comfortable.

Deanna dared to increase her speed. "Oh my word. We're flying!"

Evan raised his fists above his head like he was on a roller coaster. "Woo-hoo."

She giggled at him. "Thank you for taking time off to teach me. The ranch is really coming along. When do you think you'll be ready to start accepting boys who need help?"

"Not sure. Even though I'm enrolling as a subsidiary under the organization that ran the ranch I attended, there's still a lot of legal hoops to jump through. I'm hoping it might be approved for occupants by summertime."

"Oh!" Deanna tightened her grip on the steering wheel.

"What's wrong?"

"There's a car coming."

Up ahead, a silver sedan approached on the other side of the road. It was traveling much faster than their measly forty miles an hour and would probably pass them soon. Her neck shrank down into her shoulders. She directed the wheel to the right. The tires hit rough pavement. The truck wavered.

"Easy." Evan's voice remained calm. He didn't grab the wheel from her but laid a hand on her arm. "You don't have to give him your lane, too. This one belongs to you. Stay in the center and own it."

"But—"

"Don't worry. He sees you."

Deanna allowed the truck to drift to the middle of the right lane. The silver car whizzed past without the driver even glancing their way. She exhaled.

"Great job." Evan patted her arm before letting go.

The "Hallelujah Chorus" played through the speakers, and Deanna laughed. "Did you choose the soundtrack?"

"Nope." He laughed along with her. "It was meant to be." He pointed to a small cul-de-sac about a half a mile ahead. "Why don't you make a U-turn there, and we'll head back to town?"

Deanna gulped. She slowed to a mere ten miles an hour as she entered the turnaround, drove in a half circle, and scanned from the right to the left. Easing onto the other lane, she pointed the truck homeward.

"I can't believe it," she crowed. "This is the longest I've ever driven. Anyone else who tried to teach me always got fed up and took over. Thank you, Evan. You've got the perfect personality to work with young men who need someone patient and compassionate to help them."

He gave an embarrassed shrug. "I'm not that patient. But I do know what it's like to be in their shoes. Hopefully, my experience will help me relate."

"Of course it will." Deanna reached and grabbed his hand while still keeping her eyes on the road. "Have you considered any more about pursuing a degree?"

His fingers clenched under hers, and she hurried to elaborate.

"Please don't misunderstand me. I think you could do a great job just the way you are. And I'm not one to talk. I never went to college either. But ..."

"But?"

"You're so good at interacting with Marco. I can imagine how you might help others if you studied counseling. Even if you choose not to, this ranch for troubled youth will be amazing. You'll be changing lives, like someone did for you. And I can't wait to see it."

"You may be the only one." He didn't pull his hand away from hers. "I've heard several people in town expressing concerns regarding the kind of so-called degenerates I'll be bringing to Sweetheart."

"Don't listen to the grumblers like Boone." Deanna squeezed his fingers. "Most people will accept what a great idea it is if you give them some time."

Evan didn't reply.

"Carol of the Bells" came through the speakers, and Deanna ding-donged along with the choir. The cheerful song filled the truck cab with holiday ambiance.

She gasped.

"What's wrong?" Evan sat straight, jerking his hand away.

"Oh my word. I just had an amazing idea! What if you threw a big Christmas party at the Double Heart Ranch for the whole town?"

"What? Hold on, Hurricane Deanna. Why would I do that?"

"People are dying of curiosity to see what you've done with the place." Deanna kept her left hand on the steering wheel and waved with her right. "We could string Christmas lights in the barn and borrow folding chairs from the church. All the citizens could come and check out the bunkhouse where the boys will stay, the way you've converted the back porch into an enclosed eating area, and the different work projects you've planned for the residents. If people can examine for themselves how organized and well thought out you have everything, they'll be more willing to trust you and maybe even want to help."

"That'll be the day."

"Yes, it will. This place is called Sweetheart for a reason. The people around here are always ready to pitch in. Take what they've done with the theater." Deanna looked his way. "They saved us months of wor—"

"Watch out!" Evan grabbed the dashboard.

She stared forward. A black-and-brown dog froze in the middle of the road. Deanna swerved. She jerked her foot to hit the brake. Her sandal shifted. It caught on the edge of the pedal, wedging between the gas and the brake. The truck zoomed forward. The dog scurried to the right and escaped into a nearby field.

"My shoe's stuck!" Deanna hollered. She tugged her foot, but the straps of her sandal held tight.

Evan undid his seat belt, snatched the pocketknife from the cup holder, and bent to the floorboard. The accelerator climbed to fifty-five, then sixty miles an hour. From the radio, the choir singers' voices rose in crescendo with their wishes of a merry Christmas.

"Oh, God, help us," Deanna shrieked.

Evan's strong fingers wrapped around her ankle. He slashed the fabric ties from her leg and pulled her free, then yanked the shoe out. Deanna hit the brake with her bare foot. The truck skidded on the gravel at the side of the road. Evan crashed into the console, his head hitting the dashboard. The truck bumped along until its right front tire dipped into a small ditch, and they stopped.

Deanna clapped a hand to her mouth. "Oh, Evan. Are you okay?" She shifted to Park and then struggled to release her seat belt. The clasp came undone, and she grabbed his face. "You're bleeding!"

He rose and turned his head to study the small cut in the rearview mirror. "It's just a scratch. No big deal."

"No big deal? I could have killed us both." She lurched away and pressed her palms to her eyes. "You got hurt because of me." Bursting into tears, she slumped in her seat.

On the radio, the frenetic bells finally ceased, and "Silent Night" took their place.

Deanna sobbed. She was anything but "calm" and "bright." Why had she ever attempted to get behind the wheel?

"Hey." Evan's arms reached around her. He drew her as close as the armrest between them would allow. Patting her back, he made soft, calming sounds. "Shhhhh. Everything's okay." He laughed. "Even the dog's okay."

She scrubbed at her tears. "How can you joke about this? I ruined your truck."

"Oh, please. This old rig's gotten way worse treatment in Dallas traffic. Believe me." Evan brushed a stray hair from where it stuck to her wet cheek and smiled. "Are you ready to drive us back to town?"

Deanna pushed him away and scrambled against the door. "Are you insane? I never want to drive anything ever again."

"That's why you have to do it." He scooted to his side of the truck. "If you don't drive now, the fear will only grow. We can take it slow. I promise I won't complain even if you drive five miles an hour the whole way back."

Deanna whimpered and wrung her hands. "Isn't there any other way?"

"Sleep in heavenly pe-eaaaace."

He picked up his phone and silenced the overenthusiastic singer. "We can do without the Christmas music."

Evan reached across Deanna to grab her seat belt. The action brought his face near hers. The skin near his blue eyes crinkled as he hovered a centimeter above her.

"Don't worry. I'll be right beside you." He clicked the belt in place and then fastened his own. "I know you can do this."

Deanna drew a shaky breath. Partly from almost dying, and partly from Evan's proximity. She laid both hands on the steering wheel, flexed her bare right foot, and placed it on the gas pedal. "Okay, but I'm praying all the way to town."

Evan chuckled. "Me too."

"Well, at least something good came from this disaster. We should have another lesson again tomorrow."

He moaned.

Deanna laughed, put the truck in Drive, and never let the speedometer rise above twenty the whole way back.

Chapter Twenty-Nine

I t hadn't felt this cold when he left the ranch. The uninterrupted glare of street lights on the dark pavement stretched as far as he could see. Not a single car had passed in the last five minutes. Evan hunched under the right side of his truck, pointed the light on his cell phone, and ran a hand along the tire tread.

"Ugh." His fingers made contact with a chunk of gum stuck in the rubber grooves, and he flinched.

Looked like Marco had been spitting his lime-green wad anywhere he pleased again. Evan moved the light around until he found a nail protruding from the lower part of the tire. The deflated rubber made it clear he wouldn't be driving any farther until it was replaced. The problem was, he'd already used the spare when he had that flat at the ranch a few days ago. Marco had been there to help him change it, but this time, Evan was on his own.

He rubbed a thumb against the nail. Pulling it out might do more damage. Better to wait in case the tire could be patched. He thumped his palm against the truck.

This was supposed to have been a quick trip into town for

more paint. Evan was about three miles outside the city limits when his warning light came on. Now he was stuck. He glared both ways on the deserted country road. The streetlights were few and far between, and not a soul was in sight. After retrieving his phone from inside the truck, he stared at the screen.

There was no one to call for a ride.

Deanna didn't drive—especially not after the fiasco that was their first lesson. Mrs. Hammington didn't own a car. And he'd been so busy working on the ranch, he hadn't forged any bonds with the other townspeople.

That wasn't exactly true.

He'd kept his distance on purpose. Some folks were kind. Some weren't. Since he never knew which reaction he was going to get, he was hesitant to start any long conversations.

He slapped the rail of the truck bed. "I guess I'm walking."

Evan popped the collar of his coat and tucked it around his neck. He struck out at a fast pace. The pavement clicked under his cowboy boots.

Fifteen minutes later, he was wishing he'd stayed in the truck. The temperature had dropped. An icy cloud expelled from his mouth when his breath hit the frigid air.

A familiar building loomed in the distance. The First Church of Sweetheart. He knew it well from the countless hours he'd spent there as a child. The landmark meant he was still a good thirty-minute walk from town.

Why was it freezing? Southern Texas winters were usually mild. A bitter gust hit him, and he shoved his hands deep into his pockets. His fingers closed around something. He withdrew a small, pink business card. Lanette's number. He'd forgotten he'd even kept it.

"No way." He crumpled it into a tiny ball.

Another blast of frosty air knocked him backward. He

groaned and dragged out his phone. His pride wouldn't keep him warm. Smoothing the card, he read the number and typed a short text.

This is Evan. I'm at your church. Can you give me a ride?

He regretted it the moment he sent it. But it was too late. The cold had gotten the better of him.

He jogged across the yard of the white clapboard church and up the porch steps. Evan huddled in front of the doors where pine wreaths hung. Electric candles sat in the windows, giving off a warm, welcoming glow. Add in a few carolers, and it could be a Christmas card.

Tree branches rustled in the darkness. The church's steeple stretched into the night sky like a finger pointing at a God he no longer trusted. Evan glared in suspicion at the wooden double doors. There's no way they'd be open this late on a Tuesday evening. But it would be a long, chilly wait if he didn't at least check. He reached for the knob. It turned in his hand.

Evan froze. It had been years since he'd crossed the threshold of a church. Would lightning strike him if he entered? Another bitter blast hit. Shaking off his misgivings, he stepped inside the building and shut the door behind him. A cozy warmth filled the vestibule. The narrow entryway was just a stopping place outside the main sanctuary, but it was enough for him. He could wait right by the door until Lanette responded.

A bulletin board to the side snagged his attention. Thumbtacks held pictures on the cork background. He moved to get a better look. Familiar faces stared at him. Aunt Lanette and Uncle Harry painting the church shed. Deanna and Katherine serving coffee. Willy Walker grasping a crying baby in the nursery. Ronnie Ford. Mr. and Mrs. Page. Susanna and Daniel holding kids resembling them. He could name every single person in front of him. It was a photo album of people from his past.

Of his family.

He stretched his neck from side to side. Pacing from one end of the room to the other ate up approximately fifteen seconds. There wasn't a single chair in the space. He chuckled as a memory played in his head. Pastor Thibodeaux had shooed people out and said, *"If you want to fellowship, there's a fellowship hall. If you want to pray, there's a prayer room. But the vestibule's for vestibuling."*

To this day, Evan still didn't know what that meant. His gaze cut to the sanctuary doors with the eye-level glass windows. How could it hurt to take a peek? Chances were, the room had been remodeled since his childhood.

He walked to the closest door and peered through the glass. Was it possible? Everything from the seats to the light fixtures remained the same. Glossy wooden pews stretched on the left and right, with a middle aisle between them. Deep red carpet lined the way. The pulpit was the thick, old-fashioned kind with a cross carved in the front, not a modern-day aluminum lectern the television preachers favored.

Without permission, his hand pushed the door open. His feet moved on autopilot. A slight ache spread through his jaw, and he realized he was clenching his teeth. Forcing himself to relax, Evan crept to the front, almost like a burglar. He settled on the pew his family had always used. The hymnal rack on the back of the pew that sat in front of him held a few offering envelopes, but nothing else.

Evan swallowed. Would it still be there?

He knelt on one knee and crouched low until his head was beneath the rack. Carved into the wood, it was faint but still legible. Two words. *Hi God.*

"Here to confess?" a deep voice asked.

Slam. Evan's head hit the narrow rack. He shot to his feet, grabbed his skull, and stared at the man who'd been the spiritual leader of his childhood.

Pastor Thibodeaux had seemed larger than life, but now Evan topped him by a good five inches. A liberal patch of gray spread through the man's close-cut black hair. His smile was exactly the same, except for a few more wrinkles around the mouth. "I always suspected you were the one who etched that message in the pew."

"Uh." Evan gulped. "Sorry about that, Pastor Thibodeaux."

"Don't think any more about it, son." The older man reached out and gripped his arm. "I was hoping you'd come and see us."

"Us?" Evan surveyed the sanctuary. "Is your wife here?"

"No. Mary's at home." Pastor Thibodeaux chuckled. "I was talking about Someone else." He pointed a finger upward.

"Ah." Evan gave a half-hearted shrug. "I don't think He'd be interested in seeing me."

"Nonsense." The pastor sat and pulled Evan down on the pew with him. "We've both missed you."

Evan focused on the altar where he'd knelt as a boy—before he'd learned how cruel life could be. The antagonistic sound that left his lips was anything but gentle. "Maybe you've missed me, but the Man Upstairs had bigger things to worry about."

"There's nothing more important to the Heavenly Father than His children. You must remember the Bible story of the Good Shepherd leaving the ninety-nine sheep to find the missing one. You even played the lost sheep in our Christmas play."

"Yeah." Evan's bitter laugh echoed in the large room. "That was perfect casting."

He couldn't look at the pastor, afraid the perceptive man

would discern in Evan's eyes all the bad choices he'd made in the intervening years. The Bible might spin comforting tales about kindly fathers welcoming home their wayward sons, but he'd stopped believing in a merciful God a long time ago. Besides, why would He even want someone like Evan back?

Pastor Thibodeaux patted him on the shoulder. "It doesn't matter how far you've wandered, Evan. I promise you, God kept your room ready and waiting."

The sanctuary doors crashed open behind them. Lanette barreled down the aisle in a purple tracksuit with pearls lining the seams, her hair in rollers, not a stitch of makeup on her face. "Evan, honey." She hurried to the end of their pew. "Are you okay?"

The two men stared at the unique sight of an underdressed Lanette Johnson. Usually, every hair was in place, and her makeup was flawless.

"I'm fine," said Evan. "I got a flat and needed a ride into town."

"Oh, thank the Lord." She pressed her heaving bosom and gasped for air. "I was in such a rush, I didn't even answer your text. I knew something bad must have happened for you to contact me. But I must say, it's good to see you in church again." Lanette touched a self-conscious hand to the curlers covering her head. "You take your time. I'll sit out in the car and keep the heater running." She exited as quickly as she came.

Pastor Thibodeaux chuckled. "That's the first time in forty years I've seen Lanette Johnson without her hair done." He stood and stretched his back. "I'm afraid I've gotten old while you were gone, Evan. You better be in that pew on Sunday, or I'll come and find you." The minister crossed the room to a door beside the platform and disappeared.

Evan studied the unchanged room. The stained glass

windows he'd observed as a child stretched to the clear glass archways overtop. Colorful scenes depicted the classics: David and Goliath, Daniel and the Lions' Den, Moses and the Red Sea. When he was a little boy, he'd believed with all his heart that God would defeat anything bad that happened.

Apparently, his father's stupidity was something even God couldn't stop.

He cringed, expecting a heavenly slap against the back of his head for the blasphemous thought, but the sanctuary remained brimstone-free. A quiet peace permeated the air, inviting him to stay awhile. Evan shook his head and shoved to his feet. Spending too much time in this church was dangerous. He might start believing in fairy tales again.

Evan walked through the sanctuary and paused at one of the front doors. He leaned his head against the wood. Why had he asked Lanette for a ride? It was sure to be torture—another exhausting round of apologies and excuses. He expelled a breath, walked outside, and got into the idling white SUV.

Lanette waited for him to fasten his seat belt, put the car in gear, and drove off. "Where do you want to go? Jake Thornton lives on the second floor of his autobody shop. I bet you can get a new tire from him."

"Sounds good," Evan said.

To his surprise, Lanette didn't say another word. They traveled down the picturesque street in silence. Red and green garland adorned the iron lampposts, and colorful Christmas lights lit the store windows. The distance that would have taken him thirty minutes to walk was finished in short order. She braked outside the repair shop and pointed at an apartment over the garage. "Jake should be there. He can help you find a replacement tire and give you a ride to your truck."

Evan opened the door and exited. Pausing with his back to her, he fought an inner battle with his conscience. One favor didn't wipe away the years of bitterness. But she'd rushed to his aid when he texted. How could he just ignore her generosity?

He turned before he lost his nerve. "Thanks for the ride. I-I appreciate it."

A soft smile crossed her face. "Anytime, sugar. Anytime."

Evan nodded and shut the door. Lanette gave him a wave and drove away. The tightly coiled angst inside of him released the slightest bit. Only a centimeter. But it felt good. Maybe someday it would unwind all the way and disappear.

He hoped so.

Chapter Thirty

C ream-colored wood gleamed under the freshly installed stage lights as Deanna swept the new floorboards. The buttery glow warmed her to the core as the scratchy sound of Christmas carols played from her portable record player in the corner. She looked out at the empty auditorium. This was the only room in the theater that qualified as halfway decent. The slanted lower floor was pockmarked from the missing seats, but at least it was clean. How long would it be before she could afford new, padded theater rows? Oh well. Folding chairs would do for the present.

She might never have had the courage to start this venture if it weren't for Evan. She must be sure to tell him that when he arrived. Deanna pursed her lips in a happy whistle. She'd only seen him once this week as he pushed to finish things for the open house at the ranch. A twinge of guilt hit her conscience. The open house had been her idea, but she hadn't helped much since the theater renovation was taking the bulk of her time.

She thumped the broom on the floor. "I'll make up for it tomorrow. The Double Heart barn will be so covered in holly and ribbon, the town will get a holiday high just standing in it."

Despite his busy schedule, Evan had promised to come and help her clean out the junk in the basement. She'd always known he was a keeper. Perhaps tonight she'd find the will to reveal her hidden secret. The longer she waited, the more cowardly she became, always wanting him to draw a little closer before she ran the risk of him spurning her forever. Regardless of the outcome, Evan deserved to know the truth.

A crack of thunder echoed from outside the building. It was getting ready to pour. She hoped he made it before the rain started.

Her phone dinged. Deanna grabbed her cell, sank down on the stage, and swung her legs over the edge. She checked her texts and found a message from him.

Can't come. Sorry.

The terse tone was unlike Evan. Had something happened?

She texted him back. *Are you okay?*

It was a minute before his response arrived. *Someone broke the bunkhouse windows. I need to cover them before it storms.*

Deanna jolted to her feet. What kind of sick person would do that? Certain people in town were nervous about the possibility of a ranch for troubled youth, but they wouldn't stoop to vandalism. Who was persecuting Evan? And why? Surely, they didn't hold a grudge because of what his father did all those years ago.

She jumped off the stage and raced toward the front doors. Reaching the main entrance, she ran outside. Thunder boomed. Deanna slapped a hand to her forehead. It was almost sunset, and the sky rumbled again like it was about to pour buckets. Definitely not bike-riding weather.

But how could she leave Evan alone at the ranch? It took him years to work up the courage to return to Sweetheart. If he suspected someone was trying to drive him away, it might crush him.

Lightning flashed. Deanna looked at the darkened clouds and snorted. She wasn't scared of storms. What she feared the most was Evan deciding that staying in Sweetheart wasn't worth it.

She squeezed her eyes shut and prayed. "God, have You got a chariot of fire You can lend me?"

EVAN PICKED THE JAGGED SHARDS OF GLASS FROM THE GROUND WITH his work gloves. He was running out of time. The debris from three windows would scatter in the storm if he didn't get it cleaned up. He sifted through the mess for the large pieces. The smaller fragments could be sucked up with a shop vac. His fingers stuck to something, and he bent closer to take a look.

Oh boy. He hadn't been searching for clues, but there it was.

A heavy wind rattled the oak tree limbs around the bunkhouse, and he squinted at the sky. Lightning illuminated how many clouds had gathered while he worked. Any minute, the rain would start. Evan rubbed his face. This was no time for an investigation. He could process what he'd discovered once the danger ended.

He headed for the barn. If he duct-taped trash bags over the windows before the storm hit, everything else could be cleaned up later. Deafening thunder cracked above him. He quickened his steps. As he passed the house, movement by the road caught his eye. Renae's scarlet coupe turned in at the gate and bounced toward the bunkhouse.

Why would she be visiting in this weather?

He paused and studied the woman behind the wheel. It couldn't be.

The car pulled to a stop. Brittle leaves whisked along the ground as the driver's side door opened. Deanna jumped out, slammed it shut, and ran to him.

His jaw swung open. "Did you drive here by yourself?"

"Nope. It was me and Jesus, or I wouldn't have made it." She pressed her palms together. "I prayed out loud the whole way."

"Why are you in Renae's car?"

"I asked her to drive me, but she was swamped at work. She let me borrow the car but threatened me within an inch of my life if it gets a single scratch."

A thick gust of air knocked them both to the side.

Evan laid a hand on her shoulder. "This weather isn't fit for man or beast. Why in the world would you put yourself through that?"

"I couldn't leave you alone after something so terrible happened." She grabbed both his arms. "Are you okay?"

Evan stared at her.

Deanna shook him. "Evan Colter, are you okay?"

"I'm fine." He didn't know what else to say. She'd faced her biggest fear to come check on him. He should thank her, but what came out instead was, "What are you doing here?"

The merciless wind lashed her blonde locks against her cheeks, and she pushed them away. "I can't believe someone was cruel enough to destroy your hard work. Don't they realize how many people this will help? Don't they see it will change lives? Aggghhhh!" Her agitated hands raised and clenched into fists. "I'd like to knock whoever it is off their feet." The porch light illuminated the tears in her eyes. She sniffled and wiped her lashes. "Tell me how to help."

Evan took in the beautiful woman who had followed him

without question since they were children. He hadn't a clue what he'd done to deserve such devotion, but he felt totally unworthy. It was Deanna's unselfish and wholehearted acceptance that suddenly made him wonder if God hadn't completely abandoned him. What other explanation could there be for such undeniable love?

It was a miracle.

"Evan." She stepped closer. "What can I do?"

"Just keep being you." He grinned. "And help me tape up the windows."

DEANNA CROSSED THE RANCH HOUSE LIVING ROOM, SQUEEZING THE water from her ponytail. She sat on the pink floral couch Mrs. Hammington had been kind enough to leave behind. The room itself was sparse, with a television against the wall and a few cardboard boxes shoved together to form a makeshift coffee table. Her attention wandered from the stone fireplace to the exposed wooden beams overhead. She could do wonders with this room. Candles on the mantel. A couch and armchairs upholstered in a warm tartan pattern. Perhaps a wildlife painting by a local artist on the wall.

Evan entered and tossed her a towel. Deanna caught it and rubbed her rain-soaked hair.

"Thanks for your help out there," he said.

"I'm glad we got the windows covered before the storm hit. That would have been a mess to clean up. What are you going to do? Leave the plastic up? The open house is tomorrow."

He collapsed beside her on the couch and leaned his head on the cushion. "I don't want Mrs. Biddle and her friends asking a lot of questions, so I'll probably uncover them and hope everyone assumes I haven't installed the windows yet."

Deanna turned his way and tucked one leg up under her. "I'll stop by the store and buy extra pine garland. We can create fancy borders around the open spaces that make them look intentional."

He smiled at her. "What would I do without you?"

She winked. "Marry me, and you'll never have to find out."

He chucked her under the chin, then heaved a weary sigh.

Deanna reached to touch his arm. She rubbed the sleeve of his shirt. "I'm sorry about the windows. How could anyone be this twisted? Especially in Sweetheart. Don't they realize what a great thing it is you're planning?"

His expression was sad, like a boy who'd been bullied on the way home from school. He laid his fingers over hers. There was still a trace of moisture on them. She took the towel and dried his hand. Rubbing the soft terry cloth across each finger, she concentrated on her task. When Deanna looked up, Evan's face was pointed toward her. He studied her. Silent.

She released him and shifted against the couch cushions. "Do you have any idea who the vandals are?"

"Unfortunately, I do."

"Really?" She scooted nearer. "Who is it? Why would they do such a thing?"

Evan kept his mouth closed, and Deanna poked him.

"You're not seriously trying to go all brooding-man-of-few-words, are you?"

"I'll tell you. But not right now. I need to gather more facts first."

"Fine. If you think I'm going to beg, you're wrong." She pursed her lips in an exaggerated pout.

Evan nudged her with his shoulder. He tilted his head her way until they were only an inch apart. This close, she could spy the dark rim around his blue eyes. Her heartbeat kicked into fifth gear. She tensed and eased back.

His brows dipped. He moved away and cleared his throat. "I have an awkward question to ask."

"Oh, good." She gave a cheeky grin. "I thought the evening was too somber. An awkward question should liven it right up."

"When I first got to town, you were a little handsy."

"Excuse me,"—she held up an index finger—"stop right there. *Handsy* implies a certain level of depravity. I always conduct myself like a lady."

Evan chuckled. "Forgive me. I'll rephrase. When I first got to town, you were—"

"Choose your next words carefully."

"A very affectionate but ladylike person."

"That's better."

"But I've noticed a change in you lately." Evan cocked his head and studied her. "You don't take advantage of me anymore."

"I beg your pardon?" Deanna started to rise from her seat.

He smirked. "I'll rephrase again. You don't take advantage of the *situation* anymore. For example, last night when the Walkers and I were helping at the theater, there was a sprig of mistletoe, as big as life, above the auditorium doors, but you scooted past as if it were poison ivy. And when Elise dragged you back and pointed it out, you gave me a chaste kiss on the cheek."

She averted her gaze. "Weren't you the one who just called me a ladylike person?"

"You're a lady who never misses an opportunity for a smooch. What changed?"

Deanna pleated the towel on her lap. Her manicured fingers pinched the material and smoothed it again. "I suppose, although I might be completely wrong, it all began with the beard."

"The beard?" Evan rubbed his smooth cheek.

"To be more accurate, the *lack* of beard. When you shaved for our Shakespeare play, it kind of threw me for a loop. I'd forgotten how good-looking you were under that scruff."

"Are you saying I was ugly when I had the beard?"

"Of course not! You were still handsome as all get-out, but maybe ... more approachable."

He snorted and shook his head. "I'll never figure you out if I live to be a hundred."

Rain pelted the roof above them in a noisy shower. The wind howled, rattling the living room windows with its force. Still much too dangerous to be driving home. Was now the perfect opportunity to have the difficult conversation she'd been putting off? But how did a person start a gut-wrenching confession? Somehow, "Did you know your life was ruined because of me?" didn't have the right ring to it. Better to approach the topic from a roundabout route.

Deanna hesitated. "Now it's my turn to ask an awkward question."

Evan's tone remained unconcerned. "Fire away."

"Are you pointing out my lack of physical affection because you miss it? Or do you find it a relief?"

"That's two questions."

She slapped his shoulder. "I'm serious. You said I"—she made air quotes—"'took advantage of you.' It's important for me to know if you're teasing or if that's how you really saw it."

"Why? Will you promise to behave yourself?"

Deanna winced. "I'm not sure if I'd go that far, but I can promise to try." She looked him dead in the eye. "Please tell me if it bothers you. If you truly see me as your little sister, then I'll —I'll—"

Evan quirked his head. "You'll ...?"

She pushed herself from the couch and paced to the other

side of the room. "I started that sentence without thinking it through, and now I'm not sure how to end it. If my kisses annoy you, then I should stop. But"—she held her hands to both sides, fingers spread wide—"I guess I've always believed if I loved you hard enough, you wouldn't be able to help loving me in return."

"Looks like you weren't too far off."

"What?" She halted midpace and stared at him. "What did you say?"

That teasing grin that both delighted and annoyed her appeared again. "Nothing." He rose and crossed the room, then took her hands in his. "But, I admit, I'm happy with the way things are between us. You don't have to go changing anything."

What did that mean exactly? If he didn't want her to change, then he didn't mind her flirtatious ways. But did he also mean he didn't want to take things any deeper? Wrinkles bunched on her forehead as she analyzed his words like a high school algebra problem.

If he was coming around to the romantic side of things, perhaps it wasn't the ideal time to own up to her childhood sins.

He ducked his head to observe her closer. "That's not the reaction I was expecting. I assumed you'd do one of your old-fashioned dance steps. Why do you look so perturbed?"

"I ..." She should just do it. Admit everything. "I need to tell you—" She grasped his hands and stared into his unsuspecting face. "It's been hard for you because—"

"Don't worry about who broke the windows, Deanna. I'll take care of it."

Oh, right. The windows. Hadn't Evan been through enough tonight? She shouldn't pile more problems onto his already full plate. It was kinder to wait a little longer.

She sighed. "I'll come over bright and early to make sure the decorations are gorgeous for the open house."

"Come over?" He laughed. "You haven't left yet."

She crossed her arms. "And I want to make one thing clear. When the rain stops, you're following me back to town. I have to return Renae's car, but I don't have to do it alone. In the meantime, I've got sixty feet of Christmas ribbon in your guest bedroom. It's the perfect time to create some bows for the barn."

Deanna ignored his groans and went to fetch the ribbon. Was she being wise or cowardly to put off her big confession again? The truth was a ticking time bomb. She had to tell him. And she would.

Someday.

Chapter Thirty-One

Evan lugged the last sawhorse decoration to the drive in front of the ranch. He set the rustic reindeer on the ground, then rolled his shoulders. Marco placed an identical reindeer on the other side.

"Let's take a break," Evan called.

They walked together to the house, and Marco waited on the porch while Evan grabbed two sodas from the kitchen fridge. When he returned, they sat on the steps, popped the tops on their cans at the same time, and took a drink.

Evan inspected the winter wonderland Deanna had dreamed up. The sawhorse reindeer lined the road from the gate. Pine garlands wound around the new fencing where people would park, and giant red and green bows the size of wrecking balls graced the open barn doors. Holiday music drifted from inside, where the warm glow of twinkle lights reflected against the fresh hay sprinkled on the ground.

The boy beside him stretched out his legs and crossed them at the ankles.

"You did good work assembling the reindeer," Evan said.

"Thanks." Marco gave a half smile and took another swig. "It wasn't that hard."

"Still. It's amazing how fast you pick up on things. I only have to show you once. Perhaps you should consider becoming an architect as a career path."

"You think I'm good enough?" Marco turned his dark eyes Evan's way.

"Better than good. You've got a natural ability when it comes to building."

The teen graced him with a full smile this time. "I hate books and school and stuff. But this kind of work is okay. It feels good when I do it."

Evan gazed at the ground and twisted the soda can in his hands. "If it feels good, why did you break the windows on the bunkhouse?"

Even though he wasn't looking at the boy, he felt Marco's body stiffen beside him.

"What do you mean?" the teen asked.

"I wish I could deny it. You've helped so much around the ranch that I thought you'd take too much pride in your work. But I found a wad of gum on the ground the night the windows were broken."

"Uh"—Marco shifted—"that was from before."

"No." Evan sighed. "It wasn't. After you left yesterday, I made sure to clean all around the bunkhouse. The whole town will be coming out here today, and I wanted it to be spotless." He waited for a response, but Marco picked at his cuticles. "Is it because your aunt made you work here when you didn't want to? Or maybe you're mad at me for something."

Marco didn't answer for a long time. When he did, his voice was thick. "I'm not ... mad at you."

"So why help install the windows, then break them? Explain it to me."

The teen shoved off the steps and stomped a few feet away, kicking at the dirt. "What's the point? You're just gonna throw me out anyway."

"Says who?" Evan stood, careful to keep his distance but giving Marco his full attention. "You messed up. No denying. But I'm willing to give you another chance if you can help me understand."

"You mean"—Marco turned—"you're not going to call the police or hit me or—or make me pay you back?"

"Oh, you'll have to reimburse me." Evan smiled. "I've already calculated how much the replacement windows cost. You can work off the debt until it's paid in full. How does twenty bucks an hour sound?"

The boy's mouth quivered. His face crinkled, and he scrubbed his sweatshirt sleeve over his eyes. "I don't get it. Why would you do that?"

"I already told you. You're good at your job. Besides,"—Evan moved to stand beside Marco but directed his focus to the pasture—"I kind of like your company. It gets awfully boring working on this stuff alone."

Marco snorted. "Deanna never leaves you alone for long."

Evan laughed. "That's for sure."

"You aren't gonna tell her what I did, are you?"

"No. But *you* should."

The boy slumped. They stood side by side without speaking for a long time. A hawk soared through the sky and settled in a pine tree near the barn.

Marco broke the silence first. "I like you too. That's why I did it. Why—why I broke the windows. I was afraid once we finished the job, you'd tell me to go away."

"Pretty stupid."

"Yeah." Marco kicked a pebble, and it flicked off the nearby fence post. "Sorry."

Evan pursed his lips. He thumped the teen on the spine. "Break time's done. The whole town will be out here before we know it. Let's get to work." He took off with long strides toward the barn, and his helper scampered to his side.

The Double Heart Boys' Ranch hadn't even opened for business, but all signs indicated the old homestead was going to be a place his great-great-granddaddy would have been proud of.

Chapter Thirty-
Two

Deanna exited the barn with a sprig of mistletoe and swerved around the ladder where Evan was tacking the last piece of pine garland above the door. He descended and squinted at the salacious piece of greenery with a suspicious eye.

"Any particular reason for the mistletoe?" he asked.

"The barn requires one last, authentic, Christmassy touch." She climbed up the opposite side of the ladder he'd used and tucked the plant among the nettles and pinecones.

Evan stood on tiptoe. "It's hard to see with all the other stuff."

"Exactly." She winked down at him. "Otherwise, people might avoid it. We've got to give the single ladies like me a little help."

He placed a steadying hand on her back while she clambered to the ground and kept it there as they both took a look inside. The yuletide ambiance warmed Deanna like sitting by a fireplace with a cozy blanket on her lap. It was something out of a television holiday special. Ribbons and bells adorned the stall doors. Twinkle lights hung from the rafters. Red plaid cloths covered the tables, and a giant Christmas tree, bedecked with ornaments and candy canes, sat at the end.

Deanna entered the barn and twirled. The full skirt of her Kelly green dress swirled underneath her. "It's gorgeous."

"Are you talking about the decorations or your outfit?" Evan lounged against a supporting post.

"Both." She grabbed a large package of paper cups. "You'd better unwrap these. The visitors will be here any minute."

"We told everyone seven o'clock." He glanced at his watch. "It's only six thirty."

"Trust me. Folks in town are dying of curiosity. They'll be here early to see what we've done with the place." She exited the barn and returned a moment later, towing Marco along. "Come on. We need you to man the hot chocolate station."

"Can't I do something else?" he grumbled. "Something where I don't have to talk to people."

"No." She shoved the cups into his arms. "Learning how to hold a conversation with strangers is part of growing up. So you *will* pass out hot chocolate, and you *will* act happy about it."

She marched over to one of the tables with Marco complaining all the way, even as he followed her.

EVAN MARVELED AT DEANNA'S TALENT FOR MAKING THE GROUCHY teen cooperate. She was a beautiful pied piper in vintage clothing, able to make any man dance to her tune. And he had to agree with her. She was gorgeous in her Christmas dress with a sprig of holly and ivy adorning her artfully styled golden hair.

A rumbling drew his attention. He walked outside as a tan, four-door Oldsmobile from the eighties drove past the house. It stopped at a sign Deanna had posted along the pasture fence declaring "Reindeer Parking," and Mrs. Biddle popped out in a garish multicolored Christmas sweater, complete with flashing red and green lights.

"I couldn't wait any longer," she declared. "Tell me about this crazy plan of yours to turn the Colter homestead into an orphanage."

"It's not an orphanage," he said. "It's a boys' ranch."

Deanna hurried from the barn to join them. "That's right, Mrs. Biddle. Evan wants to help disadvantaged youth and give them a second chance at life. They'll work the land, feed the animals, and even take ballroom dancing lessons." She smirked at Evan. "At least, if I have anything to say about it."

"Sounds like a fantasy." The right side of Mrs. Biddle's mouth stretched in a disbelieving line.

"More like a dream come true." Deanna wrapped an arm around the older woman. "Come with me, and I'll give you the grand tour. We'll start with refreshments, then check out the bunkhouse, where the boys will sleep."

Mrs. Biddle shivered. "Will it take long? It's cold as an undertaker's parlor out here."

"Don't worry," Deanna propelled her into the barn, "Marco has hot cocoa waiting for you inside."

"Marco Smith?" Her penciled-on eyebrows rose. "If that's true, this place isn't a dream, it's a miracle."

"I couldn't have said it better myself." Deanna cast a secret smile at Evan as she led the nosy gossip away.

Evan expelled a breath. Would everyone who visited be as antagonistic as their first arrival?

Another vehicle lumbered down the driveaway—a large

white SUV. It parked in the spot beside the Oldsmobile, and Lanette Johnson emerged wearing black leather pants, a silver sweater, and a matching sequined cowboy hat.

For the first time since he'd returned to town, Evan was glad to see her. Even if their relationship wasn't completely mended, the way she'd ridden to his rescue on the night of the flat tire had dulled his animosity. Quiet nights at the ranch had allowed plenty of time for soul-searching, and the urge to heal and move on was strong.

"Hey there, sugar." Lanette approached him. "Your Uncle Harry had some business to finish, so he'll be coming later. It's remarkable how much you've accomplished since the last time I was out here." She surveyed the new fencing along the pasture, the freshly painted barn, and the cleaned-up front yard. "It looks great."

"Thank you." He tugged at the lapel of the green plaid dress shirt Deanna made him wear. "And thanks for the ride the other night."

"That's what family's for." She gave his arm a brief rub. "That's what you are and what you'll always be. You're my family, whether you like it or not. I hope someday you can find it in your heart to forgive me for the pain I caused you."

Evan peered at the barn doors. Deanna and Mrs. Biddle were safely hidden inside. He didn't want anyone overhearing this conversation. "I"—he cleared his throat—"I forgive you, Aunt Lanette. I admit, the memories are still there, but—but you only did what you had to."

She groaned as tears welled. "You should have warned me if you were ready to make up. I didn't wear my waterproof mascara."

He laughed. "Sorry."

"Don't be." She wrapped him in a soft hug. "It's totally worth it."

He stood stiff but accepting.

After patting his back, she released him and stepped away. "I hope being here in Sweetheart can heal you of the old bitterness."

Bitterness didn't feel like a strong enough word for the maelstrom of hurt and resentment that had plagued him for years.

Evan shrugged. "I don't understand why things had to happen the way they did—an emotional atom bomb that was dropped from Heaven. But I shouldn't have been angry at you."

"Sounds like I'm not the only one you were angry with."

"I forgive Uncle Harry, too."

"I don't mean him." Lanette swatted her hand. "I'm sure he'll be happy to hear you've forgiven him, but I meant Somebody even more important."

Evan squinted. "I don't follow."

"You're angry with God because He didn't stop your father. He allowed your dad to make his own bad choices and didn't prevent the shame and pain you and your momma experienced."

"That's ridiculous." Evan spun.

Aunt Lanette rushed to block his way. "Is it? I remember when you were a boy. You were the sweetest, most sincere thing I'd ever seen. When you said your bedtime prayers, you didn't take the easy way with the usual 'Now I lay me down to sleep.' You would spend fifteen minutes telling God all about your day and how you were feeling, and what kind of toys you wanted. You talked as if He was sitting on the bed next to you."

"So what?"

"So I wish you'd have that kind of one-on-one talk with the Almighty again."

He rolled his eyes. "What for? He's not listening."

"Sure, He is." Aunt Lanette patted him on the back. "Do you

think it was a coincidence you checked the *Clarion*'s website on the very day that story ran about the reunion? Do you think it was a coincidence Mrs. Hammington was finally ready to sell the ranch and move into town? I've been trying to convince her for years. It wasn't safe for her out here alone. But she wouldn't budge. Could it be she was holding on to the ranch until you came back?"

The hairs on the nape of Evan's neck prickled. He gaped at the sky as if he expected God to be peeking through a hole in the clouds. Of course, He wasn't.

"That was luck," he muttered.

"Luck?" Aunt Lanette scoffed. "It takes an awful lot of faith to believe so many timely things just happened to fall in line at the right second. And what about Deanna?"

"What about her?"

"She told me how you almost got in your truck and drove away that first night. Do you think it was a coincidence Deanna looked out that window at the exact moment you appeared? If she had been thirty seconds later, she'd have missed you and you'd still be in Dallas, punishing yourself for your daddy's wrongdoings."

Aunt Lanette grabbed him by the upper arms and pulled him to face her. "Wake up, sugar. The Lord Almighty is calling your name, and it's about time you answered the phone."

Evan drew a shaky breath. "What if He hangs up on me?"

"Impossible." She shook her head. "Parents love talking to their kids."

He tried to swallow the red-hot coal in his throat, but it grew, burning the back of his eyeballs. Evan blinked over and over. He was too old to cry like a little boy with a scraped knee.

Aunt Lanette's gentle smile appeared. She hugged him close and patted his back. "I've missed you so much. And I know God has, too. You gave *me* another chance. You should do the same for Him."

His chest quaked. His lips trembled, and he pressed them together. Could he do it? Was there anything left in his broken, jaded soul that could muster enough faith to believe again?

Chapter Thirty-Three

The body heat from two hundred townspeople packed in a barn chased away any hint of a winter chill. Deanna's shoes jingled as she walked. The red-and-green heels had a small golden bell sewn to each toe. Correction. One toe. She'd lost a bell somewhere in the crush.

Deanna walked among the crowd with a platter of frosted Christmas cookies and gingerbread men. She stopped in front of Katherine and her sister-in-law, Victoria Zimmerman, the elementary school principal. Deanna had been a bridesmaid with Victoria for Katherine's wedding, but she didn't know her well. The former New Yorker with her sleek black bob still retained a refined, big-city vibe, even in jeans and a simple pink sweater.

Victoria took in her surroundings with wide-eyed interest. "This is my first time in an actual barn."

"What?" Deanna stared. "Haven't you lived here a year now?"

"Yes, but I spend most of my time at school or at home."

Katherine chose a gingerbread man from the tray. "Or

traveling to Dallas with your husband to attend the symphony."

Deanna made a face. "I imagine Sweetheart doesn't offer much musical stimulation for a classical music buff."

"It helps being married to a trained musician," Victoria said. "Andrew pulls out his cello and plays for me whenever I ask. And speaking of marriage, I heard you and the new owner of this ranch are engaged. Congratulations."

"Oh, um"—Deanna fiddled with the festive gold parchment paper lining the cookie tray—"thank you."

Katherine gave her the stink eye. "You're going to have to fess up one of these days."

Victoria's curious gaze took them both in, but Deanna preferred to save any embarrassing confessions for a less populated venue.

Katherine grabbed another cookie. "These are delicious. If there are leftovers, can I take a few home?"

Victoria's husband joined their group and put an arm around his wife. "Honey, Sophie insists you come see the wooden reindeer outside."

His wife smiled. "Excuse me, please. Our favorite student is calling."

The couple walked away, and Katherine sneaked another gingerbread man with an apologetic grimace. "Sorry. This pregnancy is making me crave sweets."

Deanna pursed her lips. "You ate three cookies in one sitting before you were even married, let alone pregnant."

"And you've been fake-engaged to Evan for almost two months now."

"Shhh!" Deanna scanned the room. Were Mrs. Biddle and her radar ears within fifty feet of them?

"Seriously, Dee." Katherine downed the rest of the cookie

and brushed the crumbs from her shirt. "You've got to come clean sometime."

"I know. But it has to be the *right* time."

"It's always the right time for the truth."

"Says the woman who tells it like it is, no matter how many people protest."

Katherine raised both brows.

"Sorry." Deanna studied her holiday shoes. "It's hard to admit the biggest dream of my life is just a fairy tale."

Katherine squeezed her arm.

"There you are." Evan walked to Deanna's side. "I've been outside fending off Mrs. Biddle. She's determined to get a wedding date out of me. Plus, our honeymoon destination and the names of our first two children." He pressed his hands to the top of his head.

Katherine chuckled. "I've been telling Dee she needs to inform everyone it was a misunderstanding."

Evan looked at Deanna with wide eyes.

"It's okay." She laughed. "Katherine's known for a long time."

He sighed. "I wish I could say the same for the whole town. I hate lying to them."

"Like I said before, we're not lying. We're just not revealing all the facts."

He glared at her. "And like *I've* said before, you'd make a good politician."

Katherine cleared her throat. "As the mayor of this town, I could take offense at that. I don't. But I could."

Deanna and Evan ignored her attempt to lighten the mood. They stared at each other in a tense, wordless showdown. She tried to dismiss his silent desperation, but it was impossible. He wanted a fresh start, a clean slate, with no lies or shady tactics to recall his family's past and the misdeeds that had been revealed because of her actions. Denying him the honesty he craved was cruel, especially when he was trying to introduce the town to his plans for the boys' ranch and win their support.

Her penchant for dressing in costume and pretending had gone too far. She was hurting the man she loved. No matter how much she wanted to deny the truth, it was time to end the charade.

She spun on her one-jingle-belled heels and wove through the crowd, then stopped at the very center of the room. Deanna scrambled atop a wooden crate she'd decorated with holly leaves and snow. Fake snow. As fake as her supposed engagement. It seemed a fitting place to acknowledge her sins in front of her loved ones and acquaintances.

"Attention, please." She increased her volume. "Can y'all quiet down a second?"

People stopped talking. Aunt Lanette and Uncle Harry looked up at her with expectant smiles. Mrs. Biddle bustled through the open barn doors like she was afraid to miss something.

"I have a confession to make." Deanna gulped. "Quite a few of you have been asking when the wedding is, but"—she squeezed her eyelids shut and blurted it out—"I'm not engaged to Evan Colter."

Renae Smith stepped forward. "You broke up?"

Did she have to sound so happy about it?

"No, we didn't break up." The words gushed from Deanna. "Someone misunderstood my words the first night Evan arrived in town. Although I did say I was going to marry him, that wasn't because he asked me. It was just my wishful thinking. All of Sweetheart knows I'm crazy about him. Always have been. Always will be."

She dared to glance at the back wall where Evan stood. His expression was somber. Unreadable.

Deanna continued. "If everyone will please stop pestering him about a wedding, then he'll have more time to tell you about what a great place he's building here. Most people complain about how the younger generation is headed in the wrong direction, but how many actually do something about it? With this ranch, Evan can change hundreds of lives. And I know he'd appreciate your help. Please talk to him before you leave and find out for yourselves what an amazing plan he has." How was one supposed to end a humiliating confession? She couldn't curtsy like she did at the end of the community productions. "There are more cookies and hot cocoa at the refreshment table. Feel free to help yourself. Thank you."

She stumbled off the crate, waltzed through the bystanders as if she didn't have a care in the world, and exited the side door. Shutting it behind her, she pressed cold fingers to her flaming cheeks.

Now what should she do? No bicycle. Evan had picked her up in his truck that morning. But she had to get out of here before the questions started. They'd have to be answered eventually. But not tonight. She'd even attempt driving home alone if she had a car.

"Need a lift?" a female voice asked.

Deanna spun to find Renae leaning on the corner of the barn, jingling her keys.

Trying to get me away from Evan as quickly as possible so you can have a chance?

The sarcastic quip darted through Deanna's mind. But anything would be preferable to facing Mrs. Biddle after the big confession.

"Yes, please." Deanna followed Renae to her scarlet coupe, climbed inside, and remained silent as they drove away.

If only Renae had the same inclination.

But she didn't.

"That was a doozy of a speech you made in there."

"Yeah," Deanna said. "I've been told I have a flair for the dramatic."

"To say the least."

They passed under the wrought iron sign reading "Double Heart Ranch" and turned onto the highway. Deanna risked a peek in the rearview mirror, but there was no one in sight. What had she expected, Evan running down the road, begging her to stay?

She slumped in her seat.

"He probably needs time to process things," Renae said. "You dropped a bomb in the middle of the open house. I imagine he's surrounded by a bunch of curious people and their questions right now."

"Oh my word, you're right." Deanna covered her face and moaned. "I was trying to make it easier for him, but instead, I've made it harder. Once again, I leaped before I looked. Evan must be furious."

"He'll get over it." Renae slowed for a deer crossing the road before speeding up again. "I bet he won't be able to go one day without calling you."

Deanna tilted her head and squinted at the woman beside her. "I thought you'd be happy to discover Evan and I aren't a real couple."

"Who says you're not a real couple? Just because you aren't engaged doesn't mean you're not together. Y'all have spent the last two months glued at the hip"—she snickered—"and the lips, from what I hear."

"That was all my doing."

"A man doesn't keep kissing a woman he doesn't want to kiss. Has he ever pushed you away?"

"Well ... no."

"I rest my case."

Was Renae right? Hope fluttered inside Deanna's chest. Now that the lie about their fake engagement was out of the way, could she and Evan begin a real relationship? Reality squashed the fragile optimism before it fully spread its wings. Even if Evan felt any attraction, Deanna's appeal would disintegrate when she admitted the truth about her part in his father's arrest.

Her head flopped to the side and bonked the window. Dull pain spread through her skull, but she left her aching temple pressed against the chilly glass.

"Now what?" Renae asked.

"There's something I haven't told him. Something bad. I'm afraid he can never forgive me."

"Oh, please. I seriously doubt a Goody Two-Shoes like you has any serious slipups in her past. You want to talk real skeletons in the closet? How about writing threatening notes to a rival and chucking a brick through her window? I did a thousand hours of community service for that one. So embarrassing," she muttered. "The guy wasn't even worth it."

Deanna's lips twitched. Renae's brand of pep talk might be unorthodox, but she had to admit, it was distracting. "Sounds like you love hard."

"You ain't kiddin'." Renae sighed. "If only someone could love me back the same way."

Something, or perhaps Someone, nudged Deanna's heart. She wrestled inside herself about whether or not to say anything. What if she came off as preachy? "Not to get too religious, but I know a Guy who would die for you. We sing about Him in church every Sunday."

"Yeah." Renae's usual lazy drawl hardened. "I'm not holy enough for church."

"What a coincidence. Neither am I." Deanna shifted her body to point at the lady beside her. "But that Guy we sing about would be thrilled to see you at His front door anyway."

"How about you stop worrying about my sinful soul and focus on your own problems?" Renae slowed and halted the car at a Stop sign.

Awkwardness filled the tiny space. Deanna slowly turned to face the windshield.

"Sorry," Renae mumbled. "I'm a little sensitive about church."

"No big deal." Deanna tugged at the strap of her seat belt. "As you said, I have plenty of problems of my own." She cast a glance at her companion. "But if you ever change your mind, don't be afraid to show up out of the blue. There's always a seat open next to me."

A grunt was Renae's response, and they made the rest of the drive in silence.

Chapter Thirty-Four

The persistent pain in the crinkled spot between Deanna's eyebrows begged for relief. It had pounded away since Renae dropped her off at the theater. She loosened the red and white polka-dot bandanna she'd tied over her hair when she changed into jeans. Two hours of lying spread-eagled on the floor and calling herself every synonym for "fool" she could muster had done nothing to soothe her addled mind. Perhaps manual labor might distract her from the humiliating memory of the one-woman show she'd put on at the open house. Would Evan ever forgive her?

Shaking her shoulders, Deanna surveyed the stage floor. It needed sanding before they could prime and paint it. She snorted. A few months ago, she would have had no clue what priming was. Hanging out with Evan and Marco every week had expanded her builder's vocabulary.

The house lights were off, and only the small ones above the stage illuminated her portion of the room. It gave the theater an isolated air. Grabbing a broom, she made sure the floorboards were clean. Her quick, furious strokes mirrored the pattern of her thoughts.

What was Evan doing? Had people pestered him after her big speech? Was he mad about her ambush confession?

On the bright side, at least there were no more secrets.

Correction. There was one last secret. The biggest one.

Deanna chucked the broom into the wings, and it clattered against a pile of empty paint cans.

"Someone's having a bad night." Evan's voice carried from the back of the room.

Deanna squinted into the darkness.

Arms crossed in a nonchalant pose, he leaned against the doorjamb at the entrance. He straightened and walked to the stage, but stopped just below where she stood. "Weren't we supposed to sand the floorboards together?"

"I didn't think you'd want to come after the trouble I caused at the open house."

His chin twitched. "You definitely livened up the party. It took hours to field all the nosy questions. But I have to admit, it was a relief to get things out in the open."

A weight the size of Lubbock lifted from her conscience, and the pounding in her head ceased. "You're not mad at me?"

An affectionate smile graced his handsome face. "I'm not mad at you." He motioned to her outfit. "You changed your clothes."

Deanna spread her arms and twirled. "I went full-on Rosie the Riveter for this job."

"I approve." He rolled his sleeves to his elbows and vaulted onto the stage. "Come on, Rosie. Let's knock out this job in one night." He grabbed the sander from its box, dropped to his knees, and switched it on.

To Deanna, the cheerful buzz sounded sweeter than Frank Sinatra's best love song. She took a second sander from another box and knelt a few feet away from Evan.

After twenty minutes, Deanna waved her arm, and they both turned off their machines.

"Let's take a break." She walked to a mini fridge she'd hooked up backstage, fetched two water bottles, returned, and passed one to Evan.

He twisted off the cap and took a drink as he surveyed the section they'd sanded. "If we keep this pace, we should finish this job in a few days."

"Really?" She swiped a hand across her brow, pushing away a loose curl and tucking it under her bandanna. "It still amazes me I have a stage without any holes in it. We could put on a performance right now if we wanted to!"

"Except there are no seats for the audience." Evan gestured to the empty auditorium floor.

"A minor detail. They could bring camp chairs and blankets." She tucked her unopened water bottle under her arm and clapped with excitement. "Let's call it Picnic Plays!" She bounced on her heels. "It would be a great way to make money while we're still renovating. Plus, the community theater players get a nice big stage to perform on. What do you think?"

Evan set his bottle on a nearby table, knelt, and retrieved his sander. "I think you're dying to test these new footlights out."

She laughed. "You know me too well."

"You got that right. How can someone be the exact same person now that she was twenty years ago?"

Deanna's smile faded. "Is that a bad thing?"

"Hardly." He switched on the machine and sanded the boards with smooth, efficient strokes. "It's a comfort that there's at least one person in the world who won't let me down."

Her heart cracked at his matter-of-fact tone. How much

pain had he carried around since their idyllic childhood days ended? She got down on one knee and hovered close.

He silenced the machine, noted her unusual position, and grinned. "You're not going to propose again, are you?"

For once, she didn't answer as if it were a joke. "Only if you promise to say yes."

He clicked his tongue. "We couldn't confuse the whole town. You just informed everyone of our fake engagement tonight. They might not believe us a second time. Isn't it crazy that the mess started because we didn't want to disappoint Mrs. Hammington?"

Deanna swallowed. "About that. I kind of ... have a confession to make. I told Mrs. Hammington I planned to marry you."

Evan leaned back on his heels and quirked an eyebrow. "Aren't confessions supposed to be about something the other person *doesn't* know?"

"No, I mean, I told her I planned to marry you *after* I made it clear we weren't getting married. That the whole engagement rumor Mrs. Biddle was spreading was a farce."

Evan stood. "You told her we weren't getting married? Before she sold me the ranch?"

"Sort of." Deanna rose. "She didn't let me get the actual words out, but I got the feeling she was wise to us. And I also made it plain that I was going to do everything in my power to get you to stick around and make me Mrs. Colter." She slapped her forehead. "Wow. That sounds crass when I put it in those words. I did it because I love you, not because I'm desperate to get married. I want to fight with you in the kitchen and watch the sunset together on the porch. I want to decorate that side room of the ranch house as a nursery. And, of course, I want to kiss you in the morning and the evening and all the times in between."

Why didn't the man say something instead of standing there with an indecipherable expression? There wasn't a trace of horror. That was a good sign. But how had her unabashed admission hit him? Did she sound like a crazed stalker?

Deanna clasped both hands under her chin. "Please say something. Do you hate me? Do you think I was shameless for taking advantage of the situation?"

Evan inclined his head. "I might have if you told me a couple of months ago. But the truth is"—an incorrigible smile appeared—"lately, I've been thinking a lifetime with you doesn't sound halfway bad."

She forgot to blink, wanting to be sure this wasn't some beautiful dream she was bound to wake from. Her voice trembled when she spoke. "A-are you saying what I desperately hope you're saying?"

Confirmation shone in his soft expression. His eyes sparkled with an intimate and, dare she hope, passionate emotion she'd never seen from him.

He reached out and eased the bandanna from her head. Her hair cascaded onto her shoulders, and he buried a hand deep in the curls. With his other hand, he pulled her against him. His mouth met hers before she could form a sentence. She lost herself in his kisses as one quickly followed another. When he finally inched away, she stared, breathless as if she'd danced the Lindy Hop.

"Was that what you had in mind?" he asked.

"Oh, no," she gasped. "That was so much better."

Evan laughed and pushed a strand of hair from her forehead. "Glad to hear it. Imagine what we could do with a little practice."

"I'm all for practice." She snuggled closer.

Euphoria enveloped her, but the nagging voice of her conscience prodded again. Hadn't she confessed enough tonight? She tried to push it away, but it insisted in silent, accusing tones. Would he still want to kiss her if he knew what she'd done?

"What is it?" Evan studied her. "What's wrong?"

"Hmm? Nothing." Was the man a mind reader?

He tipped her chin with one finger. "A minute ago, you were happy as a kid at the county fair, but now you look more like you just threw up on the Tilt-A-Whirl."

Deanna scowled. "Not exactly the most romantic description at this moment."

"Sorry." He grinned, but his gaze held a question.

"Actually,"—Deanna stiffened—"I have a confession to make."

"Another one?" He laughed. "Maybe I should sit down."

Her answering laugh was weak. "Maybe you should." She removed herself from the tempting warmth of his embrace and walked to the other side of the stage. "I've debated how to tell you this. Or if I should even say anything. Part of me worries that it's dredging up painful memories." She paced to his side and laid a tentative hand on his arm. "But I couldn't live with myself if you found out from someone else. I know the scandal with your dad was the worst time of your life."

An almost tangible wall dropped between them at the mention of his father. The muscles beneath her fingers tensed. "What is there to talk about? It's in the past. Dead and buried."

"Is it? Because I suspect you think about it all the time. That it influences every major decision you've ever made." Deanna pushed the hair from her face and tromped across the room. "And I feel responsible."

His forehead knit, eyebrows dipping low. "How could you possibly be responsible for my dad's miserable choices?"

"No, not that." Deanna drew in a lungful of air and

whispered a silent prayer. "But—but your father went to jail because of me."

Even as the words left her lips, she wanted to yank them back. Why did she bring this up tonight? She ought to have waited until he was more in love with her.

Evan stood center stage, his back ramrod straight. He didn't say a word. Just stared at her.

Could she hear the air in the room? Past the auditorium doors, a car backfired on the street. The lack of speech amplified every other sound. Should she tell him the whole story or wait until he asked?

Evan spoke through tight lips. "Would you mind repeating that?"

A shiver shook Deanna to her core. This was going to hurt both of them. Why, oh why, had she brought it up tonight, of all nights?

She tried to clear the sudden knot in her throat. "It's my fault your dad got caught."

"How?" Dread laced his tone.

Deanna cleared her throat again, but the knot only grew. "The night your father was caught, I was at your house earlier in the evening. We were playing hide-and-seek. I don't expect you to remember. Anyway. While I was hiding in your dad's office, I heard him on the phone, making a plan to meet the drug dealer, a-and—" She stumbled as Evan's demeanor hardened. Her words tumbled over each other. "When I ran out into the front yard, Aunt Lanette and Uncle Harry were there and I spilled my guts and then they must have done something about it because the next morning, it was all over town your dad had been caught with criminals and then the sheriff arrested him and ..." Her voice petered out until it was a mere whisper. "I'm sorry."

"Don't be. It's not your fault." Although his words were kind, his voice was harsh, like he was biting off every sentence.

She tried to move closer, but he took a step back. Deanna froze. "Your father made bad decisions, but that doesn't change the fact that you and your mom suffered because I told on him."

"Stop." A muscle in his jaw jumped.

"I've wanted to admit it to you for years. To explain. To apologize. Maybe if I'd waited. Maybe if I had told you instead, you could have talked to your father, and he might have realized how wrong he was. I don't know how many nights I've lain awake, wondering if it could've been fixed some other way."

"I said stop!" Evan held up his hand, fingers spread wide.

Tears trickled down her cheeks. Her lips quivered. "I'm so sorry, Evan."

"I already said"—he turned away—"it wasn't your fault." He headed for the stairs that led to the lower floor. "I need to buy the new bulbs for the dressing rooms before the store closes. I'll talk to you later." He stalked along the side of the room and exited the auditorium. The door slammed behind him.

Deanna stared into the darkened room. At last, she'd admitted her shameful secret. But how had it truly gone? He hadn't railed at her or told her to get lost. Evan even said he'd talk to her later. That meant he wasn't cutting her out of his life completely. But anger had blazed from him like the scorching heat of a Texas summer. Was he being polite? Once he processed her confession, would he blame her for the pain and public ridicule he'd endured?

Her knees wobbled. She sank to the newly sanded floor and curled into a ball. What if he never spoke to her again?

Chapter Thirty-Five

I t was early. Too early. But Evan had to see Deanna. Had to explain.

He walked up the front porch steps to her house and paused at the door. Mrs. Day was an early riser. Surely, she'd be up, and she could wake Deanna. He knocked. A few seconds passed, and the door opened. But it wasn't Mrs. Day.

Deanna stood on the other side of the threshold. She wore a plain gray sweatshirt with jeans, her hair styled in a simple ponytail. As their eyes met, her body tensed. She gripped the doorjamb and stared. "Evan."

He gestured over his shoulder. "Want to take a ride with me?"

She hesitated, took a breath, and nodded. Deanna joined him on the porch and closed the door behind her. They walked to his truck, climbed inside, and Evan drove off.

Deanna never once asked where they were going. She twisted her fingers in her lap for the entire trip until the truck drove under the wrought iron sign of the Double Heart Ranch and parked outside the house.

Evan exited the vehicle, walked around the front, and

opened her door for her. He held out his hand. "Let's take a walk."

She laid her fingers in his and exited the truck. They traveled the path that led around the barn and up the back hill. A light mist meandered through the dry, winter grass of the acres of pasture stretching in front of them. Eastern meadowlarks darted across the sky, their high-pitched whistles filling the morning with music.

Deanna and Evan walked in silence, their bodies brushing. Her palm molded to his, warm and comforting. He rubbed his thumb atop hers and searched his brain for the right way to begin a difficult subject.

Evan had lain awake all night, berating himself for walking out on her at the theater. But her confession had hit too close to home. He recognized the guilty emotions she'd expressed because he shared them. It was time for some hard truth-telling. What he had to say was painful, not because she wouldn't understand, but because he didn't like to talk or even think about it. He'd never told a single soul. But she deserved to know.

"I hated my father for a long time," he began without preamble. There was no easy entrance into this conversation.

Deanna didn't reply, but her fingers tightened around his.

He continued. "Life was great. Why did Dad have to go and ruin everything? Why couldn't he be satisfied with being mayor, respected and admired? Why did he have to throw it away for money?"

The grass rustled under their feet. They approached a grove of pecan trees where a fallen log rested on the ground. Evan directed them there and waited for Deanna to sit. Once she was comfortable, he shoved his hands in his pockets and kicked at the dirt.

"Anyone would have felt that way," Deanna whispered. "It would be hard *not* to blame your father."

She gave him time to respond, but he wasn't sure what to say. Evan watched the gentle morning sunlight filtering through the branches overhead.

Deanna stood again so she was beside him. "Do you still hate him?"

"No. It took a long time to work through my anger, but we've started talking again."

"That's good." A tremor entered her tone. "Do you hate *me*?"

He honestly had no idea what she meant. "Why would I hate you?"

"Your dad was caught because of my actions. Does knowing the truth make you see me differently?"

"It wasn't because of you."

Deanna gripped his sleeve at the elbow. "Don't try to make me feel better. Go ahead and rail at me. I'd rather you let it all out. It's better than secretly resenting me."

"I don't resent you." Evan faced her. "I resent myself."

"What?" She let go of his shirt. "Why?"

Jaw tight, he raised his gaze to the sky. His words escaped through clenched teeth. "You didn't reveal my father's crimes to Lanette and Harry Johnson. They'd already heard it from someone else. Me."

Deanna wavered. She sank to the log and pressed her head. "*You* told them?"

He sat beside her, crossed his arms, and kept his eyes pointed at the ground. "You weren't the only one who overheard my dad talking on the phone that night. You probably wondered why I kept you hiding so long. Truth was, I didn't want to play hide-and-seek. We were thirteen, after all. I was resting on the bench outside of my dad's office, waiting for you to get fed up and come out on your own, when I heard through the open window what my father said. I couldn't ..." He cleared his throat. "I couldn't believe it. Dad was my hero. I wanted to be just like him. To become the mayor of Sweetheart when I was grown. But when I heard him laying out everything —the money, the drugs ... It was too plain to deny."

Deanna scooted closer and slipped her hand around the crook of his arm. "Oh, Evan." She laid her forehead against his shoulder.

"I couldn't listen anymore." He gulped. "I bolted, but the Johnsons' car was pulling into the driveway. They got out and saw me crying, and before I knew it, I'd spilled my guts."

"So when I told them about your father ..." Deanna's voice trailed away.

"They already knew. Last night, when I left the theater, I wasn't upset at your confession. But it revived a lot of bad memories. Especially when you said you wondered if you could have done something differently." He thumped the log. "I've asked myself that same question a million times. What if I had kept my mouth shut? What if I'd talked to my dad first? Asked him to stop?"

"Do you think he would have?"

"Doubtful." His bitter laugh was automatic. "My dad enjoyed expensive things too much. Still does. After he served his twelve-year prison sentence, he found a new group of wealthy friends and started schmoozing his way up the ranks."

"Where is he now?"

"San Antonio."

"He landed on his feet, right? There's no reason to blame yourself for him going to jail."

"I don't." Evan moved away from her. "He deserved what he got." After picking an empty pecan shell from the dirt, he chucked it against a tree, and it ricocheted off the trunk. "I blame myself for ruining my own life. It was the right thing to do, turning Dad in. But if I had kept silent, we could have stayed in Sweetheart. I could have grown up with my friends—with you. Sweetheart was better off without us, but I still regret the years I spent in exile as a result of my own actions." With muscles taut, he kept his back to Deanna. "Does that make me a horrible person?"

Her arms embraced him from behind. The warmth of her cheek pressed against his stiff spine. It warned him away from the black abyss of his memories.

Her voice was quiet, tender. "It makes you human. How could anyone go through what you did without becoming angry and resentful? It's natural. But you can let go of those regrets, Evan. God can help you."

"God?" He sighed. "I don't think He cares about me anymore."

"Of course He does!" Deanna tugged him around. "I'm not prepared to answer those hard questions about why God lets bad things happen and why we have to go through painful times, but I'm certain of one thing. He answers prayers. Because I prayed for twenty years you would come back to Sweetheart, and here you are." A tear streaked down her cheek. "Twenty years of not knowing where you were, how you were doing, or if you were even dead or alive. The day you walked across the school parking lot was the biggest gift God ever gave me. I felt so loved in that moment." She laid a hand over his heart. "Someday soon, I hope you can feel that way too."

Deanna drew him closer. The heat of her body enveloped him like one of Grandma Colter's homemade quilts, and Deanna's words beckoned him to believe once again.

If only he could.

Chapter Thirty-Six

The white steeple of the Sweetheart Church stood out against the bright blue sky. Folks of all ages streamed up the steps and through the open double doors.

Evan sat in his truck in the parking lot, waiting until everyone was gone. It would be easier to slip in the back once the members were inside. He tugged at the collar of his dress shirt.

Was this really a good idea?

It had been decades since he darkened the doorway of a church on a Sunday morning.

Someone tapped on his window.

He jumped and jerked his head away. A grinning Deanna stood on the other side. She made a motion for him to come out. Evan released his seat belt, opened the door, and slid from the vehicle.

"Evan Colter," she drawled in an overly thick Southern accent. "As I live and breathe. What are y'all doin' at a place like this?"

He rubbed a sweaty hand against his pant leg. "I—I thought it was about time I came to church."

"Past time." She spun him by his shoulders and pushed him toward the building. "Allow me to escort you inside."

Evan's feet dragged the closer they got to the entrance. Boone Richardson stood at the top of the steps with the welcoming air of a looming security guard. He eyed the pair of them as they approached. What if other church members had the same sour reaction? Could he face them all?

Deanna stopped pushing, came to his side, and slipped an arm around his. The simple gesture comforted him. If not for her presence, he might have left.

She studied him. "Are you ready?"

Evan nodded.

They climbed the stairs and met Boone. The cowboy took stock of Evan from his head to the tips of his dress shoes. The muscle in Boone's jaw twitched. He shoved a hand out. "Morning, Colter."

Evan blinked. "Uh, good morning." He took the other man's hand.

"I was at the open house last night." Boone gave one quick shake and released him. "Nice work with the ranch."

"Thanks."

With a curt nod, Boone went inside.

Deanna stared at Evan. "What was that about?"

He rubbed the back of his neck and laughed. "That was male speak for 'Let's be friends.'"

"Didn't sound very friendly to me. I'll never understand men."

The first strains from the organ filtered through the closed double doors.

"Come on." She pulled his arm. "The service is starting."

They entered the church, made their way through the vestibule to the sanctuary, and stood by the back. He wanted to sit in the last row, but there were no available spots. Most of the pews were full, but the one near the front where he'd sat with Pastor Thibodeaux was empty.

"Oh, good," Deanna whispered. "They saved us a seat."

She towed his unwilling body down the aisle. To his relief, there were no gasps from the other congregants. No alarm rang because an intruder was in their midst. No ushers came to escort him out. He and Deanna settled side by side on the pew, and she grabbed a hymnal from the rack. Her joyful voice joined with the other singers.

Evan dared a look around. He met eyes with Aunt Lanette on the pew opposite them, and she winked. A few pews behind sat Katherine and her husband, Ryan. She gave Evan an exasperated grimace as she wrestled with the one-year-old on her lap. Ryan took the toddler from her, and she flopped back and rubbed her swollen belly with a sigh.

Evan turned as Renae scooted onto their pew from the side aisle. The tall blonde's sheepish expression let him know he wasn't the only one feeling out of place. Deanna welcomed the woman with a hug.

On the platform, Pastor Thibodeaux beamed at Evan. His wife, Mary, sat on the organ bench, her short legs barely reaching the pedals. The choir stood in the loft behind the pulpit, clapping to the music.

Their song reached out. The old, familiar words called to him. They shoved his spirit in a time machine and transported him to his childhood, when he'd scratched the words on the hymnal rack while his mother was distracted. Life could never be that simple and protected again. But maybe it was possible to let go of the pain. Of the grief. And the constant longing.

Evan's gaze traveled to the stained glass on his right. Through the clear arched window at the top, he could see soft, expansive clouds blanketing the wide Texas sky. An impression started deep in his heart like a trickle of water breaking through the ground. It bubbled through the dry, crusty wasteland of his soul and gushed up, bringing a sensation he recognized—that sense of wonder he'd experienced as a boy.

"Hi, God," he whispered under his breath.

Deanna looked over, but he smiled and shook his head. She returned her attention to the hymnal.

A comforting warmth filled the room similar to sitting in a busy kitchen on Christmas morning. Evan could swear he smelled something sweet, not a perfume but pleasant— similar to fresh-baked bread. Were they cooking in the fellowship hall? He glanced around, but no one else seemed to notice.

Sensations rushed him. They crashed through his calm façade and pummeled him with emotions.

Regret.

Yearning.

Hope.

He breathed deep. His lungs filled with air. And for the first time in twenty years, he felt what he'd been missing.

The painful memories were still there, but the bitterness was gone. If he'd been alone, he would have huddled on the carpet and wept. But he wasn't. The woman he loved was right beside him, so crying wasn't an option. Evan absorbed the moment down to his bones.

The music drew to a close, and Pastor Thibodeaux stood at the pulpit. He spread his arms wide and bellowed in a loud voice. "Isn't it a beautiful day, friends? Our God is good, and I feel He's got one thing to say to every person in here." His benevolent face pointed straight at Evan. "Welcome home."

Evan brushed a quick hand across his eyes. The total happiness in all his years away from Sweetheart couldn't compare to this morning. He was falling backward into a fluffy snowdrift of joy. Not that he was familiar with snow. He'd grown up in South Texas, after all.

In Sweetheart.

The town where he planned to spend the rest of his life.

Chapter Thirty- Seven

Christmas carols filled the truck cab with tidings of comfort and joy. Deanna sang along with the radio as Evan drove her home from church. When they reached the house, he walked her to the front porch. She turned to him with a smile that might stretch off her face and wrapped her arms around his waist, pressing her cheek against his chest.

"I'm so happy, I might burst."

He laughed. "Why?"

"Seeing God work things out makes me want to play 'Joy to the World' on repeat. There were days and even years when I doubted you would come back." She squeezed with all her might. "I'm giddy just being able to hug you tight."

Evan encompassed her with his arms. Her small frame disappeared inside his hold. A peace and contentment radiated from him that Deanna hadn't felt since his return.

"Would you like to go on a date tonight?" he asked.

Her head poked up from his embrace. "A date? You mean a *date* date?

"I'll even bring flowers."

"Oh my word." Her cheeks burned. Evan Colter was asking her to go out with him. Finally. And it only took thirty-three years. She'd better say yes before he changed his mind. "I'd love to."

"Great. I'll pick you up here."

"That sounds wonder—no, wait!" She yanked away. "I can't."

"You can't go?"

"No. Well, yes. Sort of. What I mean is, don't pick me up here." Deanna twisted her fingers together. "Could you come to the theater instead?"

"Of course."

"Meet me in the auditorium at six. And one more thing,"— she pointed an index finger—"wait right here. I have something to give you." After fumbling with her keys, she unlocked the door and went into the house. A few minutes later, she reappeared with a large, flat box wrapped in shiny red-and-green paper. "Merry Christmas!" She extended it to him.

He took the package and raised an eyebrow. "Isn't it a little early?"

"Maybe. But I want you to wear this on our date tonight. Don't look inside until you get home."

His gaze grew suspicious, and he poked the box at her. "It's not a Santa suit, is it?"

"No." She grinned. "But don't be surprised if you find a red nose in there."

His lips twitched. "I'll keep it, but I'm not promising anything." Evan returned to his truck.

Deanna stood and watched until he was out of sight. When she could no longer see him, she sighed and squinted at the cotton candy clouds overhead. "Why tonight, God? Talk about bad timing!"

It couldn't be helped. Big plans awaited. She wasn't one hundred percent sure Evan would approve of these plans. But she had a promise to keep.

EVAN HALTED OUTSIDE THE THEATER DOORS WITH A BOUQUET OF white roses and cranberries. He smoothed his free hand down the red cable-knit sweater he'd found in the box from Deanna. It fit like it was made for him. The soft garment guarded his skin from the cool night air.

He entered the building, crossed the well-lit lobby to the auditorium doors, and opened one. Darkness filled the huge room. He searched in the gloom. "Deanna?"

She'd said the auditorium, hadn't she? He stepped over the threshold, and the lights blazed. A crowd of people waited inside.

"Surprise!" they shouted.

He took in the sea of familiar faces. People crowded into the large room, and every single one of them wore a red sweater. Aunt Lanette and Uncle Harry. Pastor and Mrs. Thibodeaux. Ryan and Katherine. Mrs. Hammington. The Walkers. The Fords. Daniel and Susanna Sheppard. The Zimmermans. Renae. They'd even talked Marco into a festive sweater. Evan couldn't imagine how.

Twinkle lights hung from the balcony. Half a dozen ornamented Christmas trees lined the sides of the stage. And in the very middle stood Deanna, wearing her own red sweater and a matching velvet-skirted dress with a white furry hem, like something out of an old movie.

She spoke into a microphone. "Evan Colter, a long time ago, I promised you the biggest welcome home party you ever saw. I'm sorry it's taken me this long to get around to it. We all wanted to get together and announce how glad we are to see you back. Sweetheart wasn't the same without you."

Mrs. H slapped him on the shoulder. "What are you waiting for, son? Go up there and get her."

Evan jogged down the sloped floor and vaulted onto the stage.

Deanna placed the microphone in a nearby stand and clasped her hands behind her, sashaying back and forth as he approached. "Are those for me?"

He extended the bouquet to her, and she squealed.

"This perfectly matches my outfit. How did you know?"

"I didn't. But you and Christmas colors go together."

"Actually, the arrangement matches both of us. Good thing you decided to wear my present. We're going to take a family picture later."

"Who is?"

"All of us." She gestured at the people filling the room. "The Sweetheart family. Now that the town's favorite son is back, it will finally be complete."

Evan looked at the rafters and drew a composing breath. "Are you trying to make me bawl in front of everybody?"

"Nope." She gave his sweater a playful tug. "Just letting you know how much I love you. How much all of us love you."

He observed the full house of partygoers. Half the town must be there—because of Deanna. He spotted a silent question in her eyes. The many years they'd spent together allowed him to guess the direction of her thoughts. Although she'd laid her heart bare for him many times, he himself had never actually said the words. It should be obvious, but women needed to hear those things.

"Yes, Deanna Day." His smile faded to something somber and sincere. "I love you. And not just in the friendly way I loved you in our childhood. The reason I can stand here tonight is because of you. When I was ready to turn tail and run, you welcomed me home. You've defended me in front of others who tried to hold my dad's crimes against me. And"—he took her in his arms—"even without the judo moves, you knock me off my feet." He slipped a hand in his pocket and withdrew a bunch of mistletoe. "I was saving this for later, but I don't think I can wait any longer." Holding the sprig over her head, he drew her close with his other arm, careful not to crush the roses.

She sparkled, not even a hint of embarrassment at being kissed in front of a room full of people. "This won't be like the Shakespeare kiss, will it?"

"Not a chance." He captured her mouth with more passion than all the Romeos the Sweet Shakes Weekend had ever known.

Cheers and whistles swelled from the ground floor below. The sound of a noisy cowbell registered somewhere in the back of his brain, but he couldn't be bothered to check and see who brought it. He was celebrating Christmas with his family, in the town he loved, with the woman he cherished in his arms.

Evan's soul sent a silent prayer of gratitude to Heaven. It felt good to be home.

Epilogue

Deanna stood with arms bent behind her in front of the full-length mirror. She swiped at the satin buttons, but the delicate lace sleeves of the vintage wedding dress restricted her movement. Her breath whooshed in a frustrated gush.

"Can someone help me get out of this?"

Katherine sat on the dressing room's small settee and picked a cookie from the refreshment tray. "Why are you changing for the reception?"

Renae Smith plucked at the shiny pencil skirt of her bridesmaid's dress. "I'd love to slip out of this fancy torture device and into some jeans."

"Don't you dare!" Deanna waggled a finger at her. "I caught Boone Richardson giving you the eye during the wedding. He's probably never seen you gussied up, and you've caught his interest. You both love grilling steaks. Why not get together and swap recipes? It might lead to something good."

"You think so?" The blonde's tapping toes belied her nonchalant expression. "Maybe I won't swap outfits until after the reception."

"You do that." Deanna made another attempt to reach her arms over her shoulders, but the too-tight sleeves made it impossible. "I, on the other hand, want out of this lace-covered prison, pronto."

"I don't get it," Katherine said. "You talked for years about wearing your grandmother's dress as you walked down the aisle. What changed your mind?"

"I already walked down the aisle." Deanna gasped. "Besides, Grandma Day was two sizes smaller than me, and my lungs are begging for oxygen. Now, are you going to help me or not?"

Renae took pity on her and unfastened the tiny buttons along the back of the wedding dress. Deanna retrieved a white brocade swing outfit with matching crinoline from the closet, walked behind the screen in the corner, and slipped them on.

Katherine laughed. "Only you would buy a spare wedding dress, just in case."

"I don't even need *one*." Renae flopped beside her on the couch and crossed her arms. "I'd be satisfied with a trip to the justice of the peace if I could find the right man."

Deanna walked around the screen and winked at her bridesmaids. "I waited thirty-three years to marry Evan Colter. I'm going to milk this day for all it's worth. That's the reason for the two dresses."

A knock sounded on the door, and Evan poked his head in with eyes closed. "Is it safe?"

"All clear," Deanna called.

He stepped inside with a grin. The sight of him in his black tuxedo with silk tie and crisp white shirt did funny things to Deanna's insides. The realization that this dreamboat was her husband hit her all over again. She'd get to look at his handsome face at breakfast every day for the rest of her life. The urge to break into song swelled, but she restrained it.

A cream-and-gold-patterned gift bag dangled from his fingers. "Honey, they're ready in the theater. The musicians are waiting for us to walk in."

"It was nice of Andrew Zimmerman to recruit some of his orchestra buddies from Austin."

"Don't forget, he and Victoria are making up half the group."

"Still, they had to ship in the other two. We owe them a huge favor. I bet no one else in Sweetheart has ever hosted a world-class string quartet at their reception."

Katherine stood from the couch. "You've turned into quite the penny-pincher."

"This bride and groom have two mortgages to pay," Deanna said. "Between your in-laws supplying the music and Susanna baking our cake, we saved a ton of money."

Evan cleared his throat and motioned to Renae and Katherine. "Why don't you two head outside? Your groomsmen are waiting to escort you."

Renae rose and wiggled the skirt of her dress into place. "Thanks again for asking Marco to be your best man. I never thought I'd see the day when he'd wear a suit voluntarily."

Evan waved off her gratitude. "Don't know what I'd do without him. He's worked harder these past six months than a team of men. We're on track to open the ranch for residents by autumn. I hope he'll be willing to help me initiate the new boys."

"Just try to keep him away." Renae walked to the door and opened it. "If you asked him to tattoo your name on his forehead, I bet he'd do it." She leaned to the side and checked her makeup in the mirror on the wall. "Don't bother saving a seat at the head table for me. I think I'll check out where Boone is sitting."

Katherine followed close behind. "Don't save me a seat

either. It's almost the baby's feeding time, so I'll probably miss at least half the reception. The joys of motherhood." Her contented tone softened the words. "You two don't make us wait long." She waggled her eyebrows at the newlyweds before shutting the door behind her.

Deanna motioned to the bag her new husband held. "What's that?"

Evan extended it with both hands. "A wedding present."

"From who?"

"Me."

"Awwww." Deanna took the gift and started to dig through the decorative tissue paper.

"Wait." Evan held up a finger. "Before you take a look, I'd like to say this falls into the 'something old' category. It's not expensive, but it's definitely something I've treasured through the years."

"I'm intrigued. May I open my present now?"

He nodded.

Deanna reached into the bag and plucked out a tattered envelope that had seen better days.

"Do you recognize it?" Evan asked.

She squinted. "Not really." Evan's name was scrawled on the front of the envelope with no address. But the scrolly penmanship was familiar. It was her own.

"Is this—?" She opened the envelope and discovered a piece of pink, flowery stationery inside. "Oh my word. You told me you got my letter, but I had no idea you kept it all these years." She unfolded the paper and silently absorbed the girlish words she'd penned so long ago. A blush crept across her cheeks, and she squeezed her eyes shut. "I can't finish! I really laid it on thick. No wonder you never answered."

"It was enthusiastic, to say the least." He took the letter from her and read aloud. "'I miss you first thing in the morning and last thing at night before I fall asleep. The days are endless without you.'"

She shrieked and covered her face with her hands. "Please don't torture me. I was fifteen. It's excruciating how pathetic I sounded."

"Pathetic?" Evan lowered the paper. "On the contrary. This letter saved my life."

"What?" Deanna peeked out from behind her fingers.

"My cousin gave me this letter right before I was sent to the ranch for rehabilitation. Everything felt worthless at the time. Like there was no point in trying. Then I read your words, and they hit me in the heart. Reminded me who I was, where I came from. Do you remember what you wrote in the last paragraph?"

"I was too embarrassed to read 'til the end."

"You said, 'Sweetheart is your home, Evan. Don't forget that. I don't care what your dad did.'" His eyes took on a faraway glint, and he quoted without looking at the paper. "'When you're ready, come back and I'll be waiting. Everyone will be waiting. We'll throw the biggest party you ever saw.'"

Deanna stared in wonder at the letter. "I can't believe you kept it."

He caught her to him. The gift bag dropped to the floor. "I knew if I ever came back, it would be great blackmail material."

She took the letter, slid her hands up the lapels of his tuxedo, and wrapped her arms around his neck. "This note may be better blackmail for me than you."

His mouth pursed. "I don't follow."

"What kind of fifteen-year-old boy keeps a sappy letter from a girl he considers a little sister?"

"I told you. I needed those words."

"That makes sense. But to hold on to it for so many years"

—she sucked air through her teeth—"I don't know. Where did you store the letter?"

"My wallet."

"Seriously?" She squealed with delight, tugged his head down, and planted a giant kiss on his lips.

When they broke apart, he regarded her with confusion. "How does that make a difference?"

"All those years I supposed I was mooning over your memory by myself, you were thinking about me, too. Perhaps I wasn't in such a one-sided love as I thought."

"You may be right. It took leaving to make me realize there was no one I missed more than you." He laughed. "But what does it matter? We officially became husband and wife an hour ago."

She sighed and held up her left hand, where the diamond-studded wedding band twinkled. "Mr. and Mrs. Colter. I could faint from happiness."

Evan backstepped them both toward the door. "Don't faint until after the reception. Half the town is waiting for us out there."

Deanna leaned to the side and placed the precious letter on the table. "We need to show this to our children someday. Remind me to get a frame when we return from our honeymoon."

"Honeymoon." Evan grinned. "I like the sound of that. Let's enjoy the party, and then we can hit the road. I'll even let you drive."

"Don't you dare!" Deanna wiggled out of his hold. "I know I've kept us out of the ditch in my last few lessons, but I'm not quite ready for a crowd of spectators watching me."

He reached behind his back, grasped the knob, and opened the door a crack. "No need to fret. I think you can handle the special ride I arranged." He disappeared for a few seconds, then returned wheeling a bright red, two-seater bicycle. A basket hung from the front with white roses spilling from the top, and a noisy string of tin cans rattled from the rack on the back.

"Oh my word." Deanna covered her mouth. "It's a bicycle built for two! Just like in the movies. I've never seen one in real life."

Evan jiggled a lever on the handle, and a cheery bell rang. "I figured this was more your speed and a lot more romantic than the truck." He lowered the kickstand. "Let's leave the reception in style. There will probably be a whole line of your ex-boyfriends out there, crying into their Stetsons."

"Please allow me to say just one more thing, my dear husband." Deanna grasped his lapels.

"Yes, my dear wife?"

"In my thirty-three years on planet Earth, I only wanted to marry you. You're the strongest, bravest, kindest, most remarkable man I know." She winked. "*And* you have the bluest eyes."

"So you really married me for my eyes?"

"Mm-hmm. I hope all six of our kids inherit them."

"Six!" He gulped. "You never mentioned that number."

"Does it bother you?"

"No. But we'd better get this reception over with, *muy pronto*. We've got some work to do." He scooped her into his arms and nudged the door open with his foot.

Deanna clasped her hands around his neck, squeezed tight, and singsonged, "Evan and Deanna, sitting in a tree, K-I-S-S-I-N-G. First comes love, then comes marriage."

He bumped his forehead against hers. "Then comes six babies in a baby carriage."

She raised a grateful look to the ceiling, but not because of the dressing room's renovated paint job. "Thank You, God. For bringing Evan back home to Sweetheart, back to me."

Evan also lifted his sight heavenward. "Ditto, God. I owe You one."

His adoring blue gaze made a circuit of her face, causing her toes to curl inside her peep-toe vintage heels. She'd waited decades for that expression, but it was worth every second.

Acknowledgments

Home. It's such a precious thing and so hard to find in this crazy world. I want to thank all of the people who have created a home for me through the years. The biggest home-makers are, of course, my mom and dad. I also want to thank all of those from my childhood that made it such a beautiful time—my Sheppard Avenue family. The sweet memories from growing up in Norfolk are some of my greatest treasures.

Thank you to Scrivenings Press for bringing the Sweetheart Series to life and to the editors who ferreted out the typos, weasel words, and parts of the story that didn't make sense: Andrea, Regina Merrick, and K. Banks.

And to the readers who have spent time in Sweetheart with me, I wish I could throw a giant Christmas party in a historic theatre to thank you all. The people who posted, and reviewed, and encouraged me along the way made the journey so much better. God bless you!

About Shannon Sue Dunlap

Shannon Sue Dunlap is a die-hard fan of happy endings and believes the Heavenly Father has designed one for each of us. She earned an M.A. in Journalism from Regent University, worked as a contributing writer for a Virginia paper, and wrote the novels *Lone Star Sweetheart, Substitute Sweetheart, Love Overboard: A Novel,* and *Hearts Aweigh.*

Inspiration comes from everywhere—including her travels, her students, and the music and movies from the golden age of Hollywood. Even in the hard times, there's humor to be found. She tries to infuse every story she writes with moments that bring a good chuckle or an all-out belly laugh. One of her greatest hopes is that readers recognize themselves in her books since everyone is the hero or heroine in their own story.

Lone Star Sweetheart—Sweetheart Series Book One

Katherine Bruno's passionate, unfiltered temper makes her the shrew of small-town Sweetheart, Texas. When she's drafted to help the mayor's wife run against her own husband, Katherine meets opposing big city political consultant Ryan Park. The good-looking, flirtatious campaign manager gets under her skin, but fraternizing with the enemy is off-limits.

Katherine must battle her lack of experience, campaign sabotage, and her growing feelings for Ryan as she strives to succeed. His unprejudiced acceptance of her strong-willed character beckons her heart, but his jaded rejection of God is an insurmountable barrier. Will Ryan return to his faith and stay with her in Sweetheart or leave when the election ends?

Get your copy here:

https://scrivenings.link/lonestarsweetheart

Substitute Sweetheart—Sweetheart Series Book Two

Buttoned-up college professor Victoria Park attends her brother's small-town wedding and indulges in a harmless flirtation with the charming and good-looking groomsman, Andrew Zimmerman. She never expected to see him again after the reception, but when Victoria is unexpectedly fired from her job, her pushy new sister-in-law recruits her as the temporary fill-in principal for the local elementary school. The unfamiliar world of tiny children and nosy employees throws Victoria for a loop, especially when she learns the beloved music teacher is none other than Andrew.

Andrew battles his disappointment when he finds the fun, attractive woman he met at the wedding has turned into a humorless, overbearing boss. He's tempted to let her flounder through the social minefields of small-town living, but there's something about Victoria that keeps him riding to her rescue. When inflammatory graffiti involving Victoria is left on the school wall, Andrew and she must work together to find the vandal and stop the ensuing gossip. The conflict draws them closer together, but will their newfound relationship hold strong when the school year ends and it's time for Victoria to return to the big-city life?

Get your copy here: https://scrivenings.link/substitutesweetheart

Much Ado about Romance

A novella collection

The Marry Wives of Sweetheart by Shannon Sue Dunlap—Mrs. Augusta Page knows best—for her daughter, Anne, and the whole town of Sweetheart, Texas. When Anne's former boyfriend, Connor Fenton, returns after many years of absence, it's a rocky road to reconciliation. Connor attempts to rekindle their romance, but Anne's wounded heart never forgave him when he left her behind for the big city.

Augusta enlists the help of her longtime buddy Veronica "Ronnie" Ford to do a little matchmaking, but obstacles abound. Her husband is against the romance, and foolish friend-of-the-family John Falstaff has taken a shine to Anne and asked for assistance. But the biggest obstacle is her daughter's stubborn heart. Mrs. Page and Mrs. Ford have their work cut out to inspire Anne Page to join the ranks of the "marry" wives of Sweetheart.

The Tempest in the Bay by Susan Page Davis—A famous writer has retreated to an island home with only his daughter. For ten years, he's hidden away and not sent his publisher any new manuscripts. His daughter Violet is now 20 and wondering if it's time for her to see more of the world since her contact with the mainland is only through

Darrell, a rather sluggish man from the shore community who brings out supplies once a month.

Paul's brother Barney and the CEO of his publisher's company set out on a yacht to track him down. But a storm intervenes, and when the sailing party lands on his island, Paul isn't sure he wants to go back.

Much Ado about Matrimony by Linda Fulkerson—Tricia Waters has resigned herself to the fact she'll never have a happily ever after, so she focuses on making her cousin's upcoming wedding a memorable one. But when she discovers her ex-fiancé is the best man, she vows to evade him. That is, until the two must work together to prevent the happy couple from breaking up.

Reeling from a personal tragedy, Dr. Ben McIntyre travels to serve as his buddy's best man only to discover the maid of honor is the love of his life. Or she was, until she ended their engagement six years earlier. He plans to keep his distance from Tricia. When circumstances keep pushing them to work together, Ben learns that avoidance is futile.

Get your copy here:

https://scrivenings.link/muchadoaboutromance

Stay up-to-date on your favorite books and authors with our free e-newsletters.

ScriveningsPress.com

www.ingramcontent.com/pod-product-compliance
Lightning Source LLC
Chambersburg PA
CBHW071554110726
47908CB00007B/2104